GENERAL CONSENT IN JANE AUSTEN

A STUDY OF DIALOGISM

Readings of Jane Austen tend to be polarized: she is seen either as conformist – the prevalent view – or quietly subversive. In *General Consent in Jane Austen* Barbara Seeber overcomes this critical stalemate, arguing that general consent does not exist as a given in Austen's texts. Instead, her texts reveal the process of manufacturing consent – of achieving ideological dominance by silencing dissent. Drawing on the theories of Mikhail Bakhtin, Seeber interrogates academic and popular constructions of Jane Austen, opening up Austen's "unresolvable dialogues."

General Consent in Jane Austen examines the "early" and "late" novels as well as the juvenilia in the light of three paradigms: "The Other Heroine" focuses on voices that challenge and compete with the central heroines, "Cameo Appearances" examines buried past narratives, and "Investigating Crimes" explores acts of violence. These three avenues into dialogic space destabilize conventional readings of Austen. The Bakhtinian model that structures this book is not one of linearity and balance but one of conflict, simultaneity, and multiplicity. While some novels fit into only one paradigm, others incorporate more than one; *Mansfield Park* receives the most attention.

A bold and provocative study, *General Consent in Jane Austen* will be of interest not only to Austen scholars but to scholars of literary theory and dialogism.

BARBARA K. SEEBER is assistant professor in the Department of English Language and Literature at Brock University.

General Consent in Jane Austen

A Study of Dialogism

BARBARA K. SEEBER

McGill-Queen's University Press
Montreal & Kingston • London • Ithaca

© McGill-Queen's University Press 2000
ISBN 0-7735-2066-x

Legal deposit third quarter 2000
Bibliothèque nationale du Québec

Printed in Canada on acid-free paper

This book has been published with the help of a grant from the Humanities and Social Sciences Federation of Canada, using funds provided by the Social Sciences and Humanities Research Council of Canada.

McGill-Queen's University Press acknowledges the financial support of the Government of Canada through the Book Publishing Industry Development Program (BPIDP) for its activities. We also acknowledge the support of the Canada Council for the Arts for our publishing program.

Canadian Cataloguing in Publication Data

Seeber, Barbara Karolina, 1968–
General consent: dialogism in Jane Austen
Includes bibliographical references and index.
ISBN 0-7735-2066-x
1. Austen, Jane, 1775–1817 – Criticism and interpretation. I. Title.
PR4037.S44 2000 823′.7 C00-900175-1

Excerpt from *Closing the Ring* by Winston S. Churchill. Copyright 1951 by Houghton Mifflin Co., © renewed 1979 by Lady Sarah Audley and the Honourable Lady Soames. Reprinted by permission of Houghton Mifflin Co.
"Aunt Jennifer's Tigers," from *The Fact of a Doorframe: Poems Selected and New, 1950–1984* by Adrienne Rich. Copyright 1984 by Adrienne Rich. Copyright © 1975, 1978 by W.W. Norton & Company, Inc. Copyright © 1981 by Adrienne Rich. Reprinted by permission of the author and W.W. Norton & Company, Inc.

This book was typeset by Typo Litho Composition Inc.
in 10.5/13 Baskerville.

Contents

Acknowledgments

Helen Vendler begins her acknowledgments for *The Odes of John Keats* by thanking Keats: "It has been a privilege (which only others who have written on Keats can fully know) to have spent a portion of my life with Keats's words and thoughts constantly in my mind." That sentence captures my feelings as I conclude this project on Jane Austen. For the past decade, her novels have been a constant in my life. To her novels, too, I owe human connections and friendships that were forged or enriched through admiration of her work. *Persuasion*'s Anne Elliot defines "good company" as "the company of clever, well-informed people, who have a great deal of conversation." Readers of Austen, I might add, are the best company.

Peter Sabor and Maggie Berg have read this manuscript at all of its various stages. Their insight, patience, and kindness have been monumental: without them, there would be no book. I owe them both the highest gratitude for supporting me, and I am fortunate to have in my life such models of the academic profession, people who combine the intellectual life with generosity of spirit. I also want to thank Juliet McMaster, Paul Stevens, John Pierce, Shelley King, and Phyllis Wright for sharing their knowledge and experience. I am grateful to McGill-Queen's University Press for making my first book a pleasant experience, and especially Joan Harcourt for believing in this book from the day that it reached her desk: thank you for being my patient guide.

An earlier version of " 'I see every thing – as you can desire me to do': The Scolding and Schooling of Marianne Dashwood" appeared in *Eighteenth Century Fiction* (11 [1999]: 223–33) and I am grateful for permission to reprint. I also want to thank W.W. Norton for permission to reprint Adrienne Rich's "Aunt Jennifer's Tigers" and Houghton Mifflin for permission to reprint a passage from Winston S. Churchill's *Closing the Ring*.

I am grateful to the Jane Austen Society of North America and the Canadian Society of Eighteenth-Century Studies.

And finally, I want to thank my mother and Darcy, my wonderful cat named after the hero of *Pride and Prejudice*.

Aunt Jennifer and Aunt Jane

~

Aunt Jennifer's tigers prance across a screen,
Bright topaz denizens of a world of green.
They do not fear the men beneath the tree;
They pace in sleek chivalric certainty.

Aunt Jennifer's fingers fluttering through her wool
Find even the ivory needle hard to pull.
The massive weight of Uncle's wedding band
Sits heavily upon Aunt Jennifer's hand.

When Aunt is dead, her terrified hands will lie
Still ringed with ordeals she was mastered by.
The tigers in the panel that she made
Will go on prancing, proud and unafraid.

Adrienne Rich

In Adrienne Rich's poem, Aunt Jennifer's needlework is a space
that facilitates subversion beneath the surface of legitimate female
activity. Rich's poem is a variation on the myth of Philomela, which
has been used as a model for women's place in society (Susan
Brownmiller in *Against Our Will*, 1975) and, more specifically, for
women's writing (Sandra Gilbert and Susan Gubar in *The Madwoman in the Attic*, 1979). Her tongue cut out, so she could not tell
her story, Philomela silently stitched a quilt that narrated her rape
and sent it to her sister, who took revenge. While Aunt Jennifer's

needlework is a tale of usurpation of male power, the poetic frame for the needlework captures Aunt Jennifer's oppression: her "fingers fluttering ... / Find even the ivory needle hard to pull," for "Uncle's wedding band / Sits heavily upon Aunt Jennifer's hand."

The Jane Austen museum in Chawton, UK, contains the famous quilt that Austen, her mother, and sister Cassandra worked on together. Comparisons have been made between Austen's needlework and the balance and detail of her novels. More significantly perhaps, both activities are presented as reassuringly feminine and detached from the (masculine) "world out there." As Carolyn G. Heilbrun states in *Writing a Woman's Life* (1988), Austen "has long been read for what she can offer of reassurance and the docile acceptance of what is given" (14).

I choose Adrienne Rich's poem as a preface to my discussion of Jane Austen because of the parallels between Aunt Jennifer and Austen. Her novel, her "little bit (two Inches wide) of Ivory" (*Austen* 1995, 323), lends itself to a conservative reading, like the tapestry created with Aunt Jennifer's "ivory needle." Yet behind the socially acceptable veneer of Gentle Jane lies an intense challenge to this construction, much like Aunt Jennifer's tigers disguised in needlework. And like those tigers, Jane Austen's novels "will go on prancing, proud and unafraid."

GENERAL CONSENT IN JANE AUSTEN

"Directly opposite notions":
Critical Disputes

∿

The Jane Austen museum in Chawton has on display the following passage from Winston Churchill's memoirs:

The days passed in much discomfort. Fever flickered in and out. I lived on my theme of the war, and it was like being transported out of oneself. The doctors tried to keep the work away from my bedside, but I defied them. They all kept on saying, "Don't work, don't worry," to such an extent that I decided to read a novel. I had long ago read Jane Austen's *Sense and Sensibility*, and now I thought I would have *Pride and Prejudice* ... What calm lives they had, those people! No worries about the French Revolution, or the crashing struggle of the Napoleonic Wars. Only manners controlling natural passion so far as they could, together with cultured explanations of any mischances. (1951, 425)

Similarly, in World War 1 hospitals Austen was recommended reading for "severely shell-shocked" soldiers (Jarrett-Kerr, in Kent 1989, 59). Christopher Kent calls this "Austen therapy" a "notable demonstration of the power of the myth of Jane Austen" (ibid.). Indeed, Churchill's letter reveals a very typical response to Austen. Her novels have often been considered curiously apolitical, hence limited; she is, in Nina Auerbach's ironic words, "the artist of contentedly clipped wings" (1985, 4). Donald Greene describes the "Myth of Limitation" as "the one steady landmark in the swirling waters of Jane Austen criticism" (1975, 142).[1] Austen's own words,

---

1 For an eloquent reformulation of this myth, see Stuart Tave: "The restrictions in the world of Jane Austen's heroines do not make their choices less significant" (1973, 33).

"3 or 4 Families in a Country Village is the very thing to work on" (1995, 275), have come back to haunt Austen scholarship.[2]

However dated, this critical tradition is very much alive. While Sybil Gloria Gross feels confident that in the 1990s, "thankfully, we are well past those genteel appraisals of Austen's achievement" (1993, 188), a perusal of recent publications on Austen tells another story. According to Roger Gard in *Jane Austen's Novels: The Art of Clarity* (1992), Jane Austen "is remarkably unpolitical for a novelist"; he adds somewhat testily, "except, of course, in the rather tiresome sense, which modern critical theorists are eager to point out on almost any occasion, that everything is in a wider way implicitly political" (15). Oliver MacDonagh's *Jane Austen: Real and Imagined Worlds* (1991) discusses how Austen's life (as revealed in her letters and family documents) is reflected in her novels: the real world is reflected in the imagined world. Both Gard and MacDonagh insist that they are not Janeites: Gard does not "want to propose a new brand of sprigged-muslin escapism, a new way of being a Janeite, or merely a Miss Austen fan" (2) and MacDonagh assures us, "Not that I am a besotted Janeite" (1991, x).

They protest too much. Both work within the construct of Austen as an unthreatening miniaturist. Gard looks at Austen as a domestic writer: "Traditional subordination and duty – most evidently that of child to parent – is, of course, present (although treated very critically), but it is a private matter and not a political factor" (1992, 16). Similarly, MacDonagh paints a picture of Austen as an accurate observer of detail. He often interjects that she did this by "instinct" (1991, 64), and he grants her so little creativity as to suggest that Catherine Morland's "rolling down the green slope at the back of the house" in *Northanger Abbey* (Austen 1988, 5:14) has its origin in Austen's own youth: "Steventon rectory no less than Fullerton Parsonage offered the necessary amenity" (MacDonagh 1991, 81). Jane Austen "did not try to be much wiser than the world at large"

2 And, as Chapman points out, the letters too are seen as limited: "A familiar complaint is that they have nothing to say about the great events that were shaking Europe – a kind of negative criticism seldom elsewhere applied to family correspondence" (1964, xxxix).

(74), thus her novels do not question or reflect on society; Jane was "obedient to the principle of the day (doubtless reinforced by the unquestioned assumptions of her father and brothers)" (80). And so we have come full circle; gentlemen from Winston Churchill to Roger Gard seem to be in perfect agreement that Austen offers us an escape from political realities.

Austen's focus on the domestic does not make her novels apolitical; for it is precisely the private matters that were the site of the ideological battles of the time. As Claudia Johnson points out in *Jane Austen: Women, Politics, and the Novel* (1988), the family was "a basic political unit in its own right" (6). In *Desire and Domestic Fiction: A Political History of the Novel* (1987), Nancy Armstrong argues that the representation of the domestic sphere translates political realities into psychological or sexual terms, so that the representation of domesticity is "a political strategy" (39). Because domestic fiction represents the individual as separate from the public world, it produced the concept of the psychologized modern individual, which in turn gave rise to the middle class. In "an age dominated by the power of discourse rather than force, by cultural hegemony rather than political revolution" (33), the idea of the individual existing separately from the political is a powerful political strategy of containment.

Marilyn Butler first recognized the political implications of Austen's representations of the domestic sphere in *Jane Austen and the War of Ideas* (1975), which contextualizes Austen in the Jacobin/anti-Jacobin debate of the 1790s, a debate that has been characterized variously as the conflict between those in favour of the French Revolution versus those "against" it; William Godwin versus Edmund Burke; the individual versus the inherited social order; radicalism versus conservatism. Butler's book not only changed Austen scholarship but also in its turn started a debate in which critics tended to be divided along party lines. Marilyn Butler, Tony Tanner, Jan Fergus, and Alistair Duckworth[3] claim that Austen is

---

3 In his introduction to the reprinting of *The Improvement of the Estate* in 1994, Duckworth, while acknowledging shifts in literary criticism, still abides by his 1971 reading of Austen as a conservative.

conservative, upholding the *status quo*, while others, such as Margaret Kirkham, Mary Evans, and especially Claudia Johnson, argue that she is subversive of the dominant ideology of her time. As Edward Neill puts it, "Currently, 'Jane' is 'Bastilled for life' by the polemics of the 1970s as well as those of the 1790s" (1991, 207).[4]

Each side of the debate tends to privilege one narrative over the other. Some critics gloss over and dismiss the texts' contradictions in order to maintain the placid surface of a conservative *oeuvre*. Often, the contradictions are interpreted as artistic failure. For example, Marilyn Butler casts the appeal of Marianne Dashwood as the problem in *Sense and Sensibility* (1811), and, rather than reinvestigate the novel's assumed conservatism, she concludes that its "moral case remains unmade" (1987, 196).

Those who read Austen as subversive, on the other hand, valorize the subtext and see the main narrative as secondary. Sandra Gilbert and Susan Gubar argue that to survive and write within her "socially prescribed subordination" (1979, 65), the woman writer developed strategies of indirection. For Gilbert and Gubar, the woman's voice lies in the "submerged meanings" (72): "women from Jane Austen and Mary Shelley to Emily Brontë and Emily Dickinson produced literary works that are in some sense palimpsestic, works whose surface designs conceal or obscure deeper, less accessible (and less socially acceptable) levels of meaning. Thus these authors managed the difficult task of achieving true female literary authority by simultaneously conforming to and subverting patriarchal literary standards" (73). As Toril Moi explains in *Sexual/Textual Politics* (1988), Gilbert and Gubar's "critical approach" is "troubling" because it "postulates a *real* woman hidden behind the patriarchal textual facade, and the feminist critic's task is to uncover her truth" (61; original emphasis).[5] Since Gilbert and Gubar locate the "true female literary authority" in the "deeper, less accessible ... levels of meaning," the main narrative is merely a

---

4 In his recent book *The Politics of Jane Austen* (1999), Edward Neill laments the "'Fogeyland' traditions of Austen critique" (10) and emphatically states the need to theorize Austen. Neill's book came out as mine was going into print.

5 Unless otherwise stated, emphasis in quotations is in the original.

"Cover Story." This has led to Gilbert and Gubar's somewhat curious preference for the juvenilia over the completed novels; for in the juvenilia Austen's "Secret Agents" (1979, 146), which constitute her "true female literary authority," are not as hidden as they are in the later writing: "Austen's adolescent fiction includes a larger 'slice of life' than we might at first expect: thievery and drunkenness, matricide and patricide, adultery and madness are common subjects. Moreover, the parodic melodrama of this fiction unfolds through hectic geographical maneuverings, particularly through female escapes and escapades quite unlike those that appear in the mature novels" (114). In *The Norton Anthology of Literature by Women* (1985), Gilbert and Gubar give "Love and Freindship" as the only example of Austen's writing. Since they include all of Charlotte Brontë's *Jane Eyre* (1847), it is clear that the choice of "Love and Freindship" [*sic*] was not simply a matter of space constraints.[6]

In *The Proper Lady and the Woman Writer* (1984), Mary Poovey also argues that the woman writer adopts stylistic strategies of indirection that "enabled women either to conceive of themselves in two apparently incompatible ways or to express themselves in a code capable of being read in two ways: as acquiescence to the norm and as departure from it" (41). As Elaine Showalter puts it in *A Literature of Their Own* (1977), "the repression in which the feminine novel was situated … forced women to find innovative and covert ways" (27–8) to express their ideas.[7] Claudia Johnson argues that "under the pressure of intense reaction," Austen "developed stylistic techniques which enabled … [her] to use politically charged material

6 Similarly, Bilger sees "unruly women" as "populat[ing] the comic landscape of Austen's juvenilia" rather than the complete novels (1998, 199): "Significantly, none of Austen's early comic efforts was published during her lifetime, and her mature fiction seldom relies upon violent comedy" (203).

7 The "feminine novel" is one of the stages in women's writing, according to Showalter. It is "the period from the appearance of the male pseudonym in the 1840s to the death of George Eliot in 1880" (1977, 13) and is characterized by the conflict between "the will to write as a vocation … [and] their status as women" (19). Although Showalter traces this conflict from the 1840s onwards, it can be dated earlier to include Austen, as, for example, Mary Poovey does in *The Proper Lady and the Woman Writer*.

in an exploratory and interrogative, rather than hortatory and prescriptive, manner" (1988, xxi). Austen "smuggle[s]" in subversive material "through various means of indirection" (xxiii, xxiv). In *Laughing Feminism* (1998), Audrey Bilger examines Austen's use of humour as a subversive strategy: "At a time when overt feminist statements could ruin a woman's reputation, comedy furnished them with a means for smuggling feminism into their novels" (11). In the introduction to a 1987 reprint of *Jane Austen and the War of Ideas*, Marilyn Butler returns to the issue of Austen's politics in light of feminist scholarship and reiterates her opinion that Austen is a conservative: "It is ... a major distraction that twentieth-century critical discourse has so firmly valorized the rebellion in the head rather than rebellion on the streets" (xlii).

I want to present a reading that overcomes this theoretical dilemma. Austen is subversive, but this subversion is not just to be situated in a barely audible subtext. Rather, it is in the interplay between main text and subtext that the subversive effect lies. As we shall see, to designate parts of the novels as subtexts is to read Austen's novels monologically; the texts themselves do not take this authoritarian stance. The theories of Mikhail Bakhtin provide a useful point of departure for this analysis.

Bakhtin's *The Dialogic Imagination* (1981) and *Problems of Dostoevsky's Poetics* (1984) use the novel as the exemplary form of dialogism, positing the site of meaning at the interaction between different voices. This relativized, multivocal meaning (dialogism), characteristic of the novel, is opposed to absolute, single-voiced, authoritative meaning (monologism), characteristic of the epic genre. To some extent, Bakhtin uses these genres as metaphors; for there are books generally called novels that he would not identify as such because they present an absolute value system and, conversely, there are poems that he would call novels. As Michael Holquist succinctly puts it, "Greater or lesser degrees of novelness can serve as an index of greater or lesser awareness of otherness" (1990, 73). Thus, when Bakhtin discusses the novel, he is referring to a relativized meaning that not only makes room for several voices but insists that the meaning lies in this network of intersecting and conflicting voices; the text, says Holquist, is the "space that gives structure to their simultaneity" (70).

While the dominant view of Austen in literary history and popular culture is still that of a quietly conservative writer, there is a growing recognition that her texts demand a more complex analysis and that Bakhtin provides a suitable avenue. Jacqueline Howard, for example, includes *Northanger Abbey* (1817) in her examination of the Gothic genre in the light of Bakhtin and argues that "Austen's parody of Gothic conventions is dialogic, pluralizing meanings and transforming official norms" (1994, 7); hence the novel "can seem extremely ambivalent" (170).[8] Yet Bakhtin is also invoked to show an Austen not very different from that of Roger Gard's. In *After Bakhtin: Essays on Fiction and Criticism* (1990), David Lodge includes a somewhat curious chapter on Austen. There is no Bakhtinian analysis, for Lodge praises Austen's novels for their

8 See Part Three for a more detailed discussion of Howard's reading of *Northanger Abbey*. Also see Roulston's discussion of gossip in *Emma*: "The circulation of gossip ... prevents the establishment of a fixed and stable monologic discourse, keeping the languages in the novel fluid and dialogic" (1996, 59). Roulston argues that while Austen "explore[s] ... a gender-based struggle for the appropriation of meaning ... she does not go so far as to acknowledge that class structures must change for the position of women to change" (61); I argue that *Emma*'s dialogism exposes class politics (see Part One). Julie Shaffer uses Bakhtin's theory of dialogism in her doctoral dissertation, "Confronting Conventions of the Marriage Plot: The Dialogic Discourse of Jane Austen's Novels" (1989). She focuses on the novels' marriage plots and argues that Austen's marriage endings are not necessarily complicit with patriarchy: "Texts that include challenges to patriarchy up until the conclusion, then, might best be viewed as carrying over the challenges to patriarchy into the marriage itself, thereby redefining the ways that marriage itself might be defined" (21). Shaffer excludes *Mansfield Park* and *Northanger Abbey* from her discussion of Austen and Bakhtin, claiming that the "challenges ... [they] make to patriarchal views of women and marriage are slight compared to the challenges made by Austen's other novels" (24). My project, of course, strongly disagrees with this approach. Gabriela M. Castellanos examines *Northanger Abbey, Pride and Prejudice*, and *Emma* in the light of Bakhtinian carnival: "What Austen did was to transpose some elements of the cultural opposition between carnival and officialdom, with carnival's characteristic mingling of many social classes, to the tension between male and female within a limited range of classes ... Her irony ... subverts dominant views of women's characters, relationships and social roles in a uniquely ambivalent way, through a laughing stance she could only have derived, albeit indirectly, from carnival" (1994, 3). Castellanos does not explore any of Austen's other novels, and her conclusions about the novels are very different from mine.

"unprecedented effect of realism" (116). Of all the novels, only
Northanger Abbey "seem[s] to deny the reader any sure ground for
interpretation and discrimination" (119); the others are decidedly
un-Bakhtinian: "It cannot be denied ... that her novels unequivocally endorse certain values and reject others. If these are grounds
for condemnation, then she stands condemned" (122). In *The
Dialogics of Dissent in the English Novel* (1994), Cates Baldridge includes *Mansfield Park* (1814) in his section on "Monologic Disrup-
tions," novels in which "the structural requirements of the genre
are at loggerheads with the text's desire to stridently endorse cen-
tripetal bourgeois discourses, and thus in which a good deal of in-
consistency and even incongruity infects the unfolding of the plot"
(10). He sees Austen's novel as an example of "conflicts between
ideological intentions and a structural imperative" (11). That in
Mansfield Park "as nowhere else in her canon, Austen champions
the middle-class desideratum of tranquility so relentlessly" (40) is a
given in Baldridge's account: dialogism is accidental – Austen cannot help but run into the dialogic, but it is only an "engagement of
a sort ... based upon flight rather than confrontation, upon distance rather than dialogue" (62).

It is not my intent to recruit Austen to a political no-woman's
land, in which ambiguities cancel out any kind of politics. The
dominant ideology strives for monologism; hence the dialogic is
subversive. Austen's dialogic texts challenge the dominant ideology, which always seeks to repress contradiction.[9]

The concept of contradiction is common to Bakhtin's theories of
dialogism and Althusser's statements about ideology. Althusser de-

9 Bakhtin's theories have proven to be particularly useful for feminist literary criticism. In *Honey-Mad Women: Emancipatory Strategies in Women's Writing* (1988), Patricia
Yaeger discusses dialogism as an "emancipatory strategy" for women writers: the dialogic
novel is "a genre that encourages its writers to assault the language systems of others and
to admit into these language systems the disruptive ebullience of other speech and of
laughter"; hence it is a form that "Austen, Eliot, Gaskell, and the Brontës chose ... because it allowed them both to disrupt a dominant literary tradition and to interrogate
their surroundings" (183). See also Dale M. Bauer's *Feminist Dialogics: A Theory of Failed
Community* (1988) and the essay collection *Feminism, Bakhtin, and the Dialogic* (1991), edited by Bauer and Susan Jaret McKinstry.

fines ideology as "*a 'Representation' of the Imaginary Relationship of Individuals to their Real Conditions of Existence*" (1971, 152) with the aim of the "*reproduction of the relations of production*" (141). This "reproduction" is achieved by two mechanisms: the "(Repressive) State Apparatus" – the government, the administration, the army, the police, the courts, the prisons – and the "Ideological State Apparatuses" – religion, education, family, legal system, political system, trade-unions, communications, and culture (141). The "Repressive State Apparatus" functions primarily, but not exclusively, by force; the "Ideological State Apparatuses," primarily, but also not exclusively, by disseminating ideology into "private" arenas and, in effect, naturalizing it. Both mechanisms have "*the function ... of 'constituting' concrete individuals as subjects*" (160). The point of this interpellation of the subject is that he or she will "naturally" and "freely" reproduce social relations: "the individual *is interpellated as a (free) subject in order that he shall submit freely to the commandments of the Subject, i.e., in order that he shall (freely) accept his subjection*, i.e., in order that he shall make the gestures and actions of his subjection 'all by himself'" (169). Althusser recognizes, however, that ideology is internally contradictory, so that there are possibilities for transformation of the ideological state apparatuses. To use Bakhtin's terms, language "is never unitary" (1981, 288); however much language aspires to monologism and univocity, contradiction is inevitable. In the interaction between different languages, we can see how ideology is ultimately always only provisional.

Althusser argues that works of art "make us 'perceive' ... in some sense *from the inside*, by an *internal distance*, the very ideology in which they are held" (1971, 204). Art (he specifically refers to "great novels," 205) in which we "are 'made to see' ideology ... has as its content the 'lived' experience of individuals. This 'lived' experience is not a *given*, given by a pure 'reality,' but the spontaneous 'lived experience' of ideology in its peculiar relationship to the real" (204–5). In other words, art draws attention to the construction of reality. A text that "permits the reader to construct from within the text a critique of this ideology" is, in Catherine Belsey's view, an "interrogative text" in opposition to the "classic realist text"

(1980, 92), which attempts to present ideology as a seamless whole and "cannot foreground contradiction" (82). Yet Belsey also points out that the denomination of a text as "classic realist" is a "choice" since "texts do not determine like fate the ways in which they *must* be read" (69). To use Belsey's word, I choose to "produce" Jane Austen's novels as dialogic and in this way to contribute to the "process of releasing the positions from which the text is intelligible" (140). The dialogic text is interrogative, for in its insistence on simultaneity and otherness, the dialogic text "foreground[s] contradiction." For example, *Sense and Sensibility* points out the contradictions in the behaviour of Elinor, who has been constructed by critics as more "sincere" than Marianne with her "artificial" sensibility. Austen's dialogic text does not privilege sense over sensibility. Rather, it explores the struggle of a particular language to achieve ideological dominance, to manufacture consent,[10] and it reveals that there is, in fact, no "general consent" (Austen 1988, 1: 378).

Just as ideology seeks to gloss over or suppress contradiction, readings of texts are carefully selective. Each reading excludes that which disrupts the chosen construction, much as it is "the role of ideology ... to suppress ... contradictions in the interests of the preservation of the existing social formation" (Belsey 1980, 45). The construction of an author is similarly selective. According to Michel Foucault, the author is "a function of discourse" (1986, 142): "These aspects of an individual, which we designate as an author (or which comprise an individual as an author), are projections, in terms always more or less psychological, of our way of handling texts: in the comparisons we make, the traits we extract as pertinent, the continuities we assign, or the exclusions we practice" (143). This discussion focuses as much on the contradictions in Austen's narratives as it does on the contradictions and exclusions in critical narratives about Austen.

Sometimes feminist criticism surprisingly produces an Austen not very different from that of Janeite criticism, one who, in the

---

10 I am borrowing this evocative phrase from Edward Herman and Noam Chomsky's *Manufacturing Consent: The Political Economy of the Mass Media* (1988).

language of traditionalists, resolves tensions or, in the more modern language of Mary Poovey, "some of the most debilitating ideological contradictions of this period of chaotic change" (1984, xvii). In Poovey's view, Austen achieves a "balance" between "her attraction to exuberant but potentially anarchic feeling" and her "investment in traditional social institutions" (182). Balance seems to be the mantra of Austen criticism; scholars as diverse as Mary Poovey, Alistair Duckworth, Kenneth Moler, Nancy Armstrong, and Glenda Hudson seem to agree on at least that much. I am proposing a reading of Austen that explores some of her "unresolvable dialogues" (Bakhtin 1981, 291).

Margaret Drabble has written that the juvenilia "provide an excellent antidote to the conventional view of Jane Austen as a calm, well-mannered novelist, confined to a narrow social world of subtle nuance and at times crippling decorum" (1989, xiv). Indeed, the inclusion of the juvenilia facilitates a more comprehensive view of Austen, one that acknowledges that her texts make room for a "whole Family" being a "sad drunken set" (Austen 1988, 6:23). It is important to note that the "sad drunken set" is not uncharacteristic of the later Austen, for *Mansfield Park*'s Mr Price "swore and ... drank" and "was dirty and gross" (Austen 1988, 3:389), particularly on the weekend: Fanny is mortified to introduce Henry Crawford to her father, "whose appearance was not the better from its being Saturday" (401).

Although in this book I focus on Jane Austen's completed novels, I also discuss parts of the juvenilia, which provide important challenges to conventional constructions of the genteel novels. Juliet McMaster has argued for the inclusion of the juvenilia in discussions of Austen. For example, in "Teaching 'Love and Freindship,'" she states that "Love and Freindship" is worthy of study for it is a "visible ... step toward the mature novels in matters of technique ... [and] theme" (1989, 150), but it also "can stand alone as a teaching text" (135). McMaster is right to suggest that if it had been "written by Byron – as it well might have been," "Love and Freindship" would "surely have been published in its own day, and read, and laughed over, and quoted, and become part of the canon" (139).

The Austen family, however, resisted publication, and it was not until 1954 that Chapman's complete edition became available.

Even today, members of the Austen family are hesitant about the worth of the juvenilia. Joan Austen-Leigh, the great-granddaughter of Jane's nephew, James Edward Austen-Leigh, "cannot help but feel that many of the earliest scraps would never have seen the light of day if they had been by another hand." She claims that Austen's "effusions of her youth, the playful, boisterous *jeu d'esprits* written to amuse her family would be of the smallest interest to the public at large" (1989, 177): "Scholars ... I venture to suspect are pretty much the only people who ever really peruse them" (178). Even some scholars have done so only grudgingly. Marilyn Butler argues that the "great majority of these short fragments seem meant for nothing more ambitious than to raise a laugh in a fireside circle" (1987, 168). For John Halperin they are "precocious and sometimes amusing but they are by no means brilliant, as those who view them with passionate hindsight like to make out – nor are they more than intermittently entertaining" (1989, 30). Others, however, argue that the minor works are worthy of attention on the grounds of their own literary merit, their relationship to the completed novels,[11] and Austen's engagement with contemporary literature and philosophy. "It is time to redress a long-standing wrong: to grant Jane Austen's early sketches more attention than they typically receive" (Johnson 1989, 45). Indeed, Austen revised parts of the juvenilia as late as 1809, which suggests that she, too, took them seriously. The debate about the worth of the juvenilia reflects the anxiety surrounding the construction of Jane Austen.

The motive of my exploration is to make sense of the contradictions and complexities that seem to riddle Austen's texts. How can her novels be seen as conservative by some and yet radically subversive by others? It is my argument that this contradiction and simultaneity, this being both conservative and radical at the same time, constitutes the dialogic nature of her work. That criticism has tried

---

11 See Fraiman's "Peevish Accents in the Juvenilia" (1993) for a particularly insightful discussion of the connections between the juvenilia and *Pride and Prejudice*.

to fix Austen on one side or other of the debate has limited her texts to half their potential meaning. My reading of Austen's texts brings to the foreground narratives that dialogize the main narratives, indeed the ones that criticism has chosen to valorize.

This book consists of three main sections. Part One, "'Some truths not told': The story of the 'other' Heroine," discusses *Sense and Sensibility, Emma* (1815), *Mansfield Park*, and *Persuasion* (1817). The stories of Marianne Dashwood, Harriet Smith, Mary Crawford, and Louisa Musgrove provide alternatives to those of the main heroines. Most criticism of these novels tends to focus on the development of the central heroine, whose happy end depends on the exclusion and silencing of her competitors. I will examine these "other" heroines as vehicles of dialogism that undermine monologic closure and interpretation. Their voices are integral to the dialogic design, "a *system* of languages that mutually and ideologically interanimate each other" (Bakhtin 1981, 47).

Part Two, "'Their fates, their fortunes, cannot be the same': Cameo Appearances," explores past narratives that are exiled from the "present" and central narrative: the story of Colonel Brandon and the two Elizas in *Sense and Sensibility*, that of Mr Elliot and Mrs Smith in *Persuasion*, and that of Wickham and Georgiana in *Pride and Prejudice* (1813). These "narrative cameos" all speak of sexual and financial exploitation that the main narrative tries to elide. Yet this subversive content cannot be contained. The stories spill over into the main narrative, disturbing the peace of the narrative that has been privileged by traditional criticism. They talk back to the central plot and reveal its inability to accommodate their stories; in this way, Austen reveals ideology as a constructed "truth." The cameos dialogize the main narrative, for they clash with the main narrative in the text, a "space that gives structure to their simultaneity" (Holquist 1990, 70).

Part Three, "'Grievous imprisonment of body and mind': Investigating Crimes," looks at *Mansfield Park* and *Northanger Abbey* in terms of a continuum and structure of violence. *Mansfield Park* explores a subtext of sexual abuse, the power structure of which pervades the whole novel, be it Fanny's continual emotional coercion or the imperialist exploitation that feeds Mansfield. The colonization of body and land is an extreme, but not disconnected, manifestation of the violence that the novel exposes. My reading of Fanny as a survivor of abuse directly contradicts the narrative that constructs her and, by extension, the novel itself as the embodiment of conservative values. Fanny's seeming acquiesence in conservative values can be seen as the programmed recital of someone living in fear, hence as the ultimate indictment of that ideology. In the section on *Northanger Abbey*, I construct a reading in which the general is guilty of the worst of Catherine's suspicions. Whether or not this interpretation is ultimately incriminating, I want to show that the possibility of Catherine's being right does exist in the text. A reading that chooses to see the possibility of Catherine's being right dialogizes the narrative that punishes and schools Catherine's imagination. The section concludes by challenging the marginal status of *Lady Susan* (1871) within the Austen canon by pointing out its similarities to *Mansfield Park*.

All three sections examine Austen's texts as dialogic. The "other" heroines, the "narrative cameos," and the "crime investigations" all are avenues into that dialogic space where contradictions flourish. In turn, my own work is dialogic, for as Bakhtin points out, "The scholarly article – where various authors' utterances on a given question are cited, some for refutation and others for confirmation and supplementation – is one instance of a dialogic interrelationship among directly signifying discourses within the limits of a single context" (1984, 188). The book's form is in keeping with its theoretical approach; the Bakhtinian narrative is not one of linearity and balance but one of conflict, simultaneity, and multiplicity. My reading does not follow the outline dryly summarized by Marilyn Butler in her analysis of 1970s scholarship: "a short introduction proposing that the Austen novels were a pinnacle of human achievement, followed by six chapters which read each of the six finished novels in loving detail" (1987, x). Even if the content has changed, the format usually has not.

My study is organized according to three paradigms (the "other" heroine, "narrative cameos," and "crime investigations"), all of which are explorations of dialogism in Austen's texts. Some novels fit into only one paradigm; others incorporate more than one. *Emma, Pride and Prejudice,* and *Northanger Abbey* are discussed in one context, whereas *Mansfield Park, Sense and Sensibility,* and *Persuasion* are discussed in more than one section. *Mansfield Park* receives the most attention because it is of special interest to me: a Bakhtinian analysis provides a particularly pertinent challenge to the common assumption that it is the most conservative and sombre of all of Austen's novels. Indeed, some of my interpretations of *Mansfield Park* seem to contradict each other. Part One posits the house of Mansfield as the site of polyphonic play, whereas in Part Three, Mansfield is the site of violence and repression. Both coexist. If my readings seem contradictory, it is because Austen's texts are. To settle on one meaning is an act of authority that the text continually defies. Hence I have partaken in, rather than resisted, the dialogic nature of Austen's novels.

"Some truths not told":
The Story of the "Other" Heroine

~

Truth is not born nor is it to be found inside the head of an individual person, it is born *between people* collectively searching for truth, in the process of their dialogic interaction.   (Bakhtin, *Problems of Dostoevsky's Poetics,* 110)

Mikhail Bakhtin begins *Problems of Dostoevsky's Poetics* (1984) with his critique of Dostoevsky scholarship as "too direct an ideological echoing of the voices of his heroes" (8). The focus on the hero "reduce[s]" the novel to "a systematically monologic whole" (9) and "has therefore been unable to perceive objectively the distinctive artistic features of Dostoevsky's new novelistic structure" (8). For Bakhtin, Dostoevsky's polyphonic novel, growing out of Menippean satire and the Socratic dialogue, is a network of ideas that meet in *"joyful relativity"* (107), rather than a system that absorbs difference under monologic authority. In the Dostoevsky novel, *"a plurality of consciousnesses, with equal rights and each with its own world,* combine but are not merged in the unity of the event." By focusing only on the hero, a reader misses the *"genuine polyphony of fully valid voices"* (6). The characters "in no way ... become principles of representation or construction for the entire novel as a whole, that is, principles of the author himself as the artist" (25). The representation of the hero's world-view as *"someone else's discourse"* (65) separate from the author and novel as a whole allows other characters and their world views to coexist. In Dostoevsky, the "idea ... becomes the *subject of artistic representation,* and Dostoevsky himself became a great artist of the idea"* (85). By "preserving a distance" (85) between the author and the hero, Dostoevsky makes us "see" ideology. As Louis Althusser points out, artists "make us 'perceive' ... in some sense *from the inside*, by an *internal distance*, the very ideology in which they are held" (1971, 204). For Bakhtin, no idea exists in a vacuum: "Every experience, every thought of a character is internally dialogic, adorned with polemic, filled with struggle, or is on the contrary open to inspiration from outside itself – but it is not in any case concentrated simply on its own object; it is accompanied by a continual sideways glance at another person" (1984, 32). Bakhtin comments on Dostoevsky's "stubborn urge to see everything as coexisting," which "explains the frequent occurrence of paired characters": "out of every contradiction within a single person Dostoevsky tries to create two persons, in order to dramatize the contradiction and develop it extensively" (28). Dialogism insists "that all meaning is relative in the sense that it comes about only as a result of the relation between two bodies occupying *simultaneous but different* space" (Holquist 1990, 20). It is impossible for anything to exist without reference to an other. This, for Bakhtin, is true of individual words and worlds.

Bakhtin's comment on Dostoevsky scholarship is relevant to Austen scholarship, much of which focuses on the development of a central heroine. In *Jane Austen and the War of Ideas*, Marilyn Butler claims that Austen "moves turn and turn about between two plots, which can be crudely characterized as built about the Heroine who is Right and the Heroine who is Wrong. The first type, the Heroine who is Right, acts as spokesman for conservative orthodoxy … The heroines who are Wrong arrive at this state of true understanding only late in the day" (1987, 166). Similarly, Jane Spencer, in *The Rise of the Woman Novelist* (1986), describes Austen's novels as part of the conservative tradition of the Reformed Heroine, and Jan Fergus, in *Jane Austen and the Didactic Novel* (1983), argues that Austen educates a central heroine and, through her, the reader. Much of Austen criticism, like that of Butler, Spencer, Fergus, Stuart Tave, Tony Tanner, Alistair Duckworth, and Walton Litz, examines the novels as *Bildungsromane*, and the values that the central heroine learns to embrace by the end of the novel are then taken to be those of Jane Austen and the novel itself. The "truth" the heroine arrives at is taken to be the novel's "truth" or ideology. This metonymic move needs to be investigated.

According to this approach to Austen's novels, the education of the heroine culminates in her maturity, her true understanding, and her marriage. Although some critics do acknowledge the potential of other world-views represented in other characters, they render them in the light of attitudes the heroine must combat to achieve full maturity or happiness. In other words, for *Mansfield Park* to end, Mary Crawford must be proven wrong and Fanny must be proven right. Mary Poovey discusses the "technique of 'doubling'" (1984, 43) as a strategy of indirection that Austen adopted in order to write "in a code capable of being read in two ways: as acquiescence to the norm and as departure from it" (41): "it provided an opportunity not only to dramatize the negative counterparts of the heroine's perfect qualities but also to play at different roles, to explore, often through the characters of servants or lower-class women, direct action forbidden to the more proper lady. Among the writers I discuss, the most accomplished mistress of this strategy is Jane Austen" (43). For Poovey, however, Austen's "doubling" is in a sense only provisional, for the text does choose one character over the other. The complexities of a situation are shown, but they are resolved. Poovey argues that Austen brackets the subversive content of her novels by displacing it onto characters other than the heroine, thus rendering it possible for the heroine to be happy within the very ideology that Austen criticizes.

Nancy Armstrong (1987) argues that Austen's "marriages ... make statements that are at once perfectly personal and perfectly political." Her heroines "marry as soon as their desire has been correctly aimed and accurately communicated" (192): "When one discovers what one wants in an Austen novel, then, the story is almost over" (193). Whereas the Brontës "broke up this congruity of personal and social experience by endowing their heroines with desire for the one object they could not possess, namely, Heathcliff and Rochester as first encountered in the novels," in Austen this is not the case: "Austen had fine-tuned the language to such a degree that there appeared to be no gap whatsoever between the behaviour of characters and their motivations by the end of each one of her novels" (192). Similarly, Poovey states, "For the most part, the culminating marriages in Austen's novels lack the undercurrents of ambivalence" (1984, 203). Armstrong's reading, like most Austen criticism, is focused on the central heroine who does indeed get to marry the man she loves.

But this kind of analysis overlooks those women who do not get the man they want, and how their desire has to be redirected and "naturally" located in someone else. Austen's closures are full of gaps that speak of the inadequacy of the endings to fulfil everyone's desire. So, Marianne Dashwood comes to love Colonel Brandon, Harriet Smith gives up her feelings for Mr Knightley and returns to Robert Martin, Mary Crawford makes an abrupt exit and Edmund quickly learns to love Fanny, while Louisa Musgrove loses interest in Wentworth and ends up with Captain Benwick. These outcomes all entail exits and silences on the part of figures who throughout the novel competed for centrality. Their stories must be exiled to the margins or come to an abrupt end for the story of the central heroine to be resolved. By leaving the plots of others unresolved, Austen's novels draw attention to the way ideology is constructed: by silencing or omitting those parts that do not fit. Thus, Austen denies ideology its naturalizing force and strips it of its power.

Positing empire as the master narrative in *Culture and Imperialism* (1993), Edward Said states that the "power to narrate, or to block other narratives from forming and emerging, is very important to culture and imperialism" (xiii). He argues for "contrapuntal reading" (66), which "must take account of both processes, that of imperialism and that of resistance to it" and which "extend[s] our reading of the texts to include what was once forcibly excluded" (66–7). This does not mean shifting the focus from what the novel is "really" about to a different narrative that current sensibility denotes as significant – that of the marginal voices. Rather, as Said points out, a "we" always presupposes a "them": "no identity can ever exist by itself and without an array of opposites, negatives, oppositions" (52). Hence, I would argue, the story in *Emma* is that of Harriet as well as Emma, because it reveals how Emma is set up as the natural superior. The suppression of other stories in *Emma* is inextricably linked to the telling of the main story; interpretation needs to look at both. Although Said does not specifically refer to Bakhtin, his argument does relate to Bakhtin's concept of polyphony. Said writes:

As we look back at the cultural archive, we begin to reread it not univocally but *contrapuntally*, with a simultaneous awareness both of the metropolitan history that is narrated and of those other histories against which (and together with which) the dominating discourse acts. In the counterpoint of Western classical music, various themes play off one another, with only a provisional privilege being given to any particular one; yet in the resulting polyphony there is concert and order, an organized interplay that derives from the themes, not from a rigorous melodic or formal principle outside the work. In the same way, I believe, we can read and interpret English novels. (51)

In his discussion of *Mansfield Park*, Said argues that "Fanny Price (and Austen herself) finally subscribes" to Sir Thomas's values (62). To argue that Austen subscribes to Sir Thomas's values is to posit polyphony as a posthumous reading strategy, rather than as a writing strategy. By showing us what the main narrative tries unsuccessfully to repress, Austen's texts incorporate challenges to the main discourse. These challenges are voiced by the "other" heroines.

    Sense and Sensibility is a *Bildungsroman* with two heroines. No other Austen novel has two heroines and this democratic two-voicedness seems to set *Sense and Sensibility* apart from Austen's typical focus on the development of a central heroine. *Emma*, the only novel that carries the heroine's name in its title, is a case in point. But the same process that is at work in *Sense and Sensibility* is also at work in *Emma*, if less overtly. And as a less-overt example, *Emma* paradoxically shows us ideology that is "working," so well in fact that the struggle of various voices does not seem to be there. In his discussion of the "depoliticization of the social subject" in contemporary American society, James H. Kavanagh (1990) points out that "declining political interest does not mean the system is not working; to the contrary, it is a sign that the system is working quite well, thank you – only working for more people more of the time

through apparatuses of ideological interpellation/subjection,
rather than those of political persuasion" (313). That the ideological battle is more visible in *Sense and Sensibility*, does not mean that
it is absent in *Emma*, *Mansfield Park*, and *Persuasion*, only that it is
more disguised. Marianne Dashwood, Harriet Smith, Mary Crawford, and Louisa Musgrove are "other" heroines whose voices reveal the limitations of the dominant ideology. Their stories contain
"some truths not told" (Austen 1988, 4:166).

Announcing herself as "a partial, prejudiced, and ignorant Historian" (ibid., 6:134), Austen is remarkably frank about this process
of exclusion in *The History of England*. In this exuberant parody of
Oliver Goldsmith's four-volume *History of England from The Earliest
Times to the Death of George II* (1771),[1] Austen "brashly inverts the
Whig view of history" (Kent 1989, 64): "Instead of arranging a conventional Whig narrative, which interpreted English history as a
gradual march towards increased liberty and as a progressive defeat
of absolutism, Jane Austen sets up history as pro-Stuart tragedy by
placing the execution of Charles I as its climax and conclusion"
(Doody and Murray 1993, 328). She constructs a history that has as
its heroine Mary Queen of Scots, not "that disgrace to humanity,
that pest of society, Elizabeth" (Austen 1988, 6:144), "my principal
reason for undertaking the History of England being to prove the
innocence of the Queen of Scotland ... and to abuse Elizabeth,
tho' I am rather fearful of having fallen short in the latter part of
my Scheme" (149). This partiality for the Catholic Stuart line is
also apparent in Cassandra's illustrations to her sister's text; Mary
looks beautiful and aristocratic, while Elizabeth definitely does
not.

"The young Jane Austen was plainly not persuaded by the novel
notion of nonpartisan history," as Christopher Kent points out
(1989, 66): "Just as history is about the exercise of power, so history
writing *is* the exercise of power." Linda Hutcheon agrees: "To write

1 The Austen family owned a copy of Goldsmith's *History*, and Deidre Le Faye points
out that "volumes III and IV bear numerous interjections and comments in the margins,
written by the youthful Jane, registering her disapproval of Goldsmith's Whig view of history and her support for the Stuart family in all its generations" (1993, x).

either history or historical fiction is equally to raise the question of power and control: it is the story of victors that usually gets told" (1988, 72). Austen creates a kind of historiographic metafiction, which challenges the division between reality and fiction and foregrounds the process of selection and narrativization of history. She refers to Nicholas Rowe's *Jane Shore* (1714), Richard Sheridan's *The Critic; Or, A Tragedy Rehearsed* (1779), and Shakespeare several times: "the King made a long speech, for which I must refer the Reader to Shakespear's Plays, & the Prince made a still longer" (Austen 1988, 6:139); and Henry the Fifth "married the King's daughter Catherine, a very agreeable Woman by Shakespear's account" (ibid.). She announces her agenda: "to vent my Spleen *against*, & shew my Hatred *to* all those people whose parties or principles do not suit with mine, & not to give information" (140). And she shamelessly promotes her own family interests: "Yet great as he [Sir Francis Drake] was, & justly celebrated as a Sailor, I cannot help foreseeing that he will be equalled in this or the next Century by one who tho' now but young, already promises to answer all the ardent & sanguine expectations of his Relations and Freinds, amongst whom I may class the amiable Lady to whom this work is dedicated, & my no less amiable Self" (146).

In her introduction to the *History*, A.S. Byatt admits that she "was rather surprised as an adult scholar to discover that Jane Austen *was* on the side of the Stuarts" (1993, vii). In Byatt's reading, Elizabeth is the "secret Heroine" (vii) of the work: "That this is possible is an indication that the young writer has difficulties with her tone. She genuinely wants sympathy for the slaughtered Queen of Scots and her grandson, Charles I, but can nevertheless continue to poke fun at them" (viii). This is not Austen having "difficulties," however, but the very strategy that we see in the completed novels. More than just reversing a power structure, the *History* allows for an alternative discourse. The "abuse" that "hardened & zealous Protestants" have given Mary for her Catholic faith Austen takes as "striking proof of *their* narrow Souls & prejudiced Judgements" (Austen 1988, 6:145). And even though Austen's sympathies lie with the Catholics, "an audaciously unusual partiality" (Doody and

Murray 1993, 332), she criticizes their behaviour during the reign of James I: "As I am myself partial to the roman catholic religion, it is with infinite regret that I am obliged to blame the Behaviour of any Member of it; yet Truth being I think very excusable in an Historian, I am necessitated to say that in this reign the roman Catholics of England did not behave like Gentlemen to the protestants" (Austen 1988, 6:147).

Austen's *History of England* affords an underdog's perspective on history, and it provides a useful point of entry into the discussion of the "other" heroines. The novels focus not only on Elinor, Emma, Fanny, and Anne but also on Marianne, Harriet, Mary, and Louisa. Like Mary, the Queen of Scots, the "other" heroine provides an alternative history, which is integral to the dialogic design of each novel, "a system of intersecting planes" (Bakhtin 1981, 48).

CHAPTER ONE

Sense and Sensibility

∾

Sense and Sensibility is often considered inferior to *Pride and Prejudice, Mansfield Park, Emma,* and *Persuasion;* in many books it is
deemed unworthy of its own chapter and is coupled with *Northanger
Abbey,* another of Austen's early attempts. Walton Litz feels confident that "most readers would agree that *Sense and Sensibility* is the
least interesting of Jane Austen's major works" (1965, 72). The
main objection to the novel is that it is too didactic and just not
convincing. According to Marilyn Butler, it "is the most obviously
tendentious of Jane Austen's novels, and the least attractive" (1987,
195). Its anti-Jacobin didacticism is very clear: "It is the role of Marianne Dashwood, who begins with the wrong ideology, to learn the
right one" (192). Elinor, representing sense, has been "right" all
along, while Marianne, representing sensibility, has to become
more like her sister. In Marilyn Butler's division of the Austen
canon, *Sense and Sensibility,* like *Mansfield Park* and *Persuasion,* belongs to the group in which the heroine "brings ... about [moral
discovery] in someone else" (166). Thus, Elinor is the "rightful"
heroine. In John Hardy's *Jane Austen's Heroines* (1984) there are six
chapters, one each for the six great heroines; Marianne is not one
of them. Similarly, for Stuart Tave, the novel is "the story of Elinor
Dashwood. The action of the novel is hers; it is not Marianne's and
it is not equally divided between the sisters: it is Elinor's" (1973,
96). Jan Fergus argues that "Austen intends that the reader's inclination to be charmed by Marianne and to be alienated by Elinor
should be subtly redirected by the text" (1983, 7). Trying to make
the novel more likeable, some readers, like Tony Tanner (1986)
and Kenneth Moler (1968), argue that both Elinor and Marianne
go through an education process, that they learn from each other,

and, therefore, that Austen proposes the reconciliation of sense and sensibility. The novel's ending, however, leaves such readers with the following dilemma: Elinor is rewarded with the object of her affections, while poor Marianne has to give up all of her dreams about the charismatic Willoughby, nearly dies, and then settles in for life with Colonel Brandon, a man who "sought the constitutional safeguard of a flannel waistcoat!" (Austen 1988, 1:378). This has led critics on both sides of the debate to assume that the problem lies with Austen as a writer, not with them as critics. Marilyn Butler claims that Austen failed to naturalize her didactic message: "In this most conscientiously didactic of all the novels the moral case remains unmade" (1987, 196). And those who argue that Austen wanted to rewrite the didactic tradition regret that unfortunately she remained trapped within its conventions.

Part of the critical problem with *Sense and Sensibility* is that it resists this pattern of reading by presenting two heroines, both appealing in their own way, who meet radically different fates. The "reader must be made to accept the priority of ... [Elinor's] moral vision," Duckworth insists, but this "task is complicated by the author's refusal in any way to limit the attractive individualism of the other sister" (1994, 114). In the other novels, "this problem is successfully avoided": while in *Sense and Sensibility* "there is a bifurcation of action and reflection, in the later novels the two modes are one in the actions and retrospective reflections of the heroine" (ibid.). The system of contrasts, however, unlike a maze that the reader, along with the heroine, has to go through to arrive at the monologic truth, represents Austen's polyphonic vision. There is a bi- or even trifurcation in *Emma* and in the other novels, too. And rather than being a "problem," "complication," or artistic failure, this is where Austen's artistic success lies. The existence of "other" heroines posits the possibility of other marriages and other truths.

A *Bildungsroman* with two heroines, *Sense and Sensibility* invites a dialogic reading,[1] yet perhaps more than any of Austen's novels, it has been seen as didactic. The pros and cons of sense and sensibil-

---

1   See Shaffer's "The Ideological Intervention of Ambiguities in the Marriage Plot" (1994) for a dialogic reading of *Sense and Sensibility*. Shaffer also argues that Austen deliberately maintains the appeal of Marianne's sensibility (rather than seeing it as a flaw), but

ity have been debated, and critics such Roger Gard, Claudia
Johnson, and Margaret-Anne Doody provide a welcome break from
this polemic. Austen's target is the "unfeeling, unintelligent world"
in which the sisters have to live, rather than the sisters themselves
(Gard 1992, 93); "given a social and financial system which is so
systematically heartless in its treatment of women ... the question
whether a young woman has 'sense' or 'sensibility' itself becomes
touched with irony" (Doody 1990, xiii). As Claudia Johnson has
pointed out, the problem lies in "those sacred and supposedly be-
nevolizing institutions of order – property, marriage, and family"
(1988, 49). While it is true that neither Elinor nor Marianne is safe
in this world, there is a pronounced inequality in the destiny of the
heroines. Elinor gets Edward and although we may find him dull,
she does not: her lot may not be as exciting as that which awaits
Elizabeth Bennet, but it is preferable to Marianne's.

Marianne comes very close to death; no other Austen heroine
undergoes such a violent education process. Although Marianne
starts out as a heroine of sensibility, she becomes a member of the
community of sense. Marianne does not successfully court her own
death during the "indulgence of ... solitary rambles" (Austen 1988,
1:303) around Cleveland, but while she recovers, she recovers only
to recant her sensibility. At the end of the novel, her individualism
is renounced and she is defined strictly in terms of her role as a
member of society: "She found herself at nineteen, submitting to
new attachments, entering on new duties, placed in a new home, a
wife, the mistress of a family, and the patroness of a village" (379).
To call *Sense and Sensibility* a novel of education is to leave out half
of the story. For obviously Marianne has already been educated, in
the school of sensibility. What is involved here is a violent purge, a

---

my conclusions are different. Influenced by Janice Radway's *Reading the Romance: Women,
Patriarchy, and Popular Literature*, Shaffer explores the role of fantasy in the novel. She argues that "the dialogic confrontation between sensibility and 'reality' ... permits readers
to recognize how fully women might desire the fantasies that sensibility provides – how
inadequate the conditions are in the extraliterary world that makes literary fantasies em-
powering women so appealing" (147) and that yet the "fantasies ... may make them inca-
pable of taking advantage of the limited satisfaction that can be theirs in this patrilinear,
patriarchal society" (148).

re-education, and a rewriting of the past. Marianne dies and is re-born, and this birth is a birth into another ideology. In a memorable phrase, Louis Althusser states that "*individuals are always-already subjects*" (1971, 164). Austen stresses that Marianne "was born to an extraordinary fate" that is not biological birth, but ideological interpellation: "She was born to discover the falsehood of her own opinions, and to counteract, by her conduct, her most favourite maxims. She was born to overcome an affection formed so late in life as at seventeen, and with no sentiment superior to strong esteem and lively friendship, voluntarily to give her hand to another! ... But so it was" (1988, 1:378). Austen presents the conversion as unlikely and anything but "voluntar[y]." That Marianne's "whole heart became, in time, as much devoted to her husband, as it once had been to Willoughby" (379) is something we never see. What we do witness is a rather violent process of manufacturing closure.

Inventing "a something ... in Willoughby's eyes ... which I did not like," Mrs Dashwood is "very sure" that Marianne "would ... never have been so happy with *him* as she will be with Colonel Brandon." Elinor "could not quite agree with her" (338) and "was half inclined to ask her *reason* for thinking so, because satisfied that *none founded on an impartial consideration* of their age, characters, or feelings, could be given" (336; emphasis added). The "pang" (339, 379) that Elinor and Willoughby continue to feel for the match that was not meant to be further underscores the contradiction at the heart of Marianne's marriage to Colonel Brandon. The text strips sense, the dominant discourse, of the power to legitimize itself. Marianne's marriage is not a natural occurrence. It needs some hefty assistance: John Dashwood, Mrs Dashwood, Elinor, and Edward "felt ... [Colonel Brandon's] sorrow and their own obligations, and Marianne, by general consent, was to be the reward of all" of Colonel Brandon's suffering. The novel asks, "With such a confederacy against her ... what could she do?" (378). Clearly, Marianne is powerless against the communal wish.

Johnson sees Austen's resurrection of Marianne as part of the novel's iconoclasm: she is "dangled over the brink of death only to be yanked back into a second and happy attachment which flies in the face of cultural ideals about women's sentimentally self-monitored loyalty to the men who first love them" (1988, 69). The happiness of the "second attachment," however, is dubious at best. Austen has Marianne defy one social convention only to enter another one. Johnson's reading, in which Marianne is allowed "to withdraw from the world" (72) and nestle happily within the privacy of the family circle, reinstates the very ideology that she argues the text unmasks: the Burkean "little platoon" (51). The novel's denaturalizing of the supposedly most natural bonds of all – family – goes beyond the unlikeableness of Mr and Mrs John Dashwood and company, for Marianne's coercion happens precisely at the hands of family members she loves.

Elinor makes sure that Marianne "submit[s]" (Austen 1988, 1:379) to her new fate. The only one who hears Willoughby's confession, Elinor decides when and how much to tell Marianne and Mrs Dashwood. Elinor "softened ... his protestations of present regard" (347) and "was carefully minute in every particular of speech and look, where minuteness could be safely indulged" (348). She is careful to "declare only the simple truth, and lay open such facts as were really due to his character, without any embellishment of tenderness to lead the fancy astray" (349). Elinor tailors the truth and paves the way for Colonel Brandon. Although a "thousand inquiries sprung up from her heart," Marianne "dared not urge one" (347–8) and resigns herself to her fate: "I see every thing – as you can desire me to do" (349). And as the newly programmed subject, Marianne recites, "I wish for no change" and then "sighed, and repeated – 'I wish for no change'" (350).

This is not to suggest that Marianne's sensibility, which is crushed out of her, was natural or even preferable. As a heroine of sensibility, Marianne follows a particular code of conduct, and as the reformed heroine, she follows another code. In both ways she is subject of a discourse. Critics often point out that Marianne's behaviour is undercut as contrived. Indeed, Marianne's behaviour is artificial in the sense that it is dictated by something bigger and outside herself, not her own unique sensibilities, as she believes. Ideology works by disguising itself as the independent, "natural" desire of individuals: Althusser tells us that "every 'spontaneous' language is an *ideological* language" (1971, 207) and that "there is no practice except by and in an ideology" (159). When we see that Marianne "would have thought herself very inexcusable had she been able to sleep at all the first night after parting from Willoughby" (Austen 1988, 1:83), we observe her replicating a predetermined code of conduct. Marianne's behaviour is clearly artificial, but not for the reasons usually given: that Austen is on the side of sense; that she has not yet outgrown the burlesque of the juvenilia; that, as Poovey suggests, she must make Marianne "seem intermittently ridiculous" (1984, 189), for "to take Marianne's passions and longings seriously on their own terms would be to call into question the basis of ... the social order" (188). Rather, the overtly dramatic Marianne is the key to the text's exposure of individual language as always already an acting out of an ideologically constituted language. This does not make Marianne's suffering any less painful or significant. We may laugh at Marianne, but we are also moved by her. That Marianne's behaviour is constructed, moreover, is only half the story. The denaturalized position of Marianne invites us to recognize how Elinor's naturalized position is manufactured.

Marianne's grief becomes ironic from Elinor's point of view, but Elinor is hardly an impartial observer. *Sense and Sensibility* does not allow us to see only with Elinor's point of view, for Austen makes us aware of gaps, omissions, and contradictions, stories that sense cannot tell, stories that do not make sense. By incorporating contradictions, Austen incorporates contrary discourses, thus giving us a glimpse of the polyphonic world that the dominant ideology, in order to legitimize its hegemony, needs to repress. Austen shows how any discourse tries to deny the validity of another discourse. To validate her own behaviour, Elinor has to undercut Marianne's. Elinor's self-righteous "I will not raise objection against any one's conduct on so illiberal a foundation, as a difference in judgement from myself, or a deviation from what I may think right and consistent" (Austen 1988, 1:81) can hardly be taken at face value in the way Jan Fergus does: Elinor "tries to allow for differences between her opinions and conduct and other people's" (1983, 47). Clearly, the novel suggests otherwise. When Marianne realizes the dangers of sensibility and Mrs Dashwood confesses "imprudence," Elinor was "satisfied that each felt their own error" (352).

Throughout the novel, Elinor polices Marianne's behaviour; on their return to Barton, Marianne

grew silent and thoughtful, and turning away her face from their notice, sat earnestly gazing through the window. But here, Elinor could neither wonder nor blame; and when she saw, as she assisted Marianne from the carriage, that she had been crying, she saw only an emotion too natural in itself to raise anything less tender than pity, and its unobtrusiveness entitled to praise. In the whole of her subsequent manner, she traced the direction of a mind awakened to reasonable exertion. (342)

Elinor observes and approves of Marianne's reformed behaviour. However, there are contradictions in this code. Marianne's emotion is "natural in itself" but subjected to "reasonable exertion." What is at stake here is not emotion but its codification. Readers who side with Elinor often remind us that Elinor has feelings too, and of course she does. But the text emphasizes that both exertion and indulgence are performances; both are directed to something or someone beyond the self; both are answers to the calling (interpellation) of ideology, be it that of sense or of sensibility.

Elinor is unaware of how she is used as a tool by the ideology of sense, and of how her affection for Marianne is recruited by the dominant ideology to secure her sister's subjection, for Elinor feels she is acting in her sister's and family's best interests. It is because of her own ideological positioning that Elinor thinks these two interests can be reconciled. Repeatedly we see Elinor attempting to find her happiness by acting in accordance with society's expectations. Elinor's self-denial is not the unequivocally heroic self-sacrifice it is often made out to be, for Elinor does get satisfaction out of "feeling that I was doing my duty" (262). Elinor's "plan of general civility" (94), however often cited as her selflessness in comparison to Marianne's selfish insistence on individual happiness, is also shown to be motivated by self-interest. The point here is neither to demonize nor to humanize Elinor but to show how her "self-lessness" is a flattering construction facilitated by discursive power: Elinor subscribes to an ideology that places individual happiness within the community; hence her behaviour is no more selfless or selfish than Marianne's, which is constituted by an individualistic ideology. For example, Elinor's offer to help Lucy complete "a fillagree basket for a spoilt child" (144) of Lady Middleton's appears to be generous. However, Elinor "joyfully profited" (145), for she receives an opportunity to satisfy her curiosity about Lucy and Edmund's engagement and "to convince Lucy ... that she was no otherwise interested in it than as a friend" (142). Thus, "by a little of that address, which Marianne could never condescend to practise, [she] gained her own end, and pleased Lady Middleton at the same time" (145). The self-gratification Elinor finds in seeming to be selfless is further parodied when she leaves the room to give Edward and Lucy Steele some privacy: "Her exertions did not stop here; for she soon afterwards felt herself so heroically disposed as to determine, under pretence of fetching Marianne, to leave the others by themselves; and she really did it, and *that* in the handsomest manner, for she loitered away several minutes on the landing-place, with the most high-minded fortitude, before she went to her sister" (241–2). Elinor's "exertions" are shown to be as contrived and staged as Marianne's indulgences. Elinor is not exempt from Austen's irony: both languages are denaturalized.

That Austen puts Elinor and Marianne in parallel situations is obvious but still instructive. Much of their behaviour is similar, but Elinor presents hers in a reasonable light. Her sister is instrumental in this process. Elinor has much at stake in portraying Marianne as overindulgent, for her own identity as a women of sense depends on it. For someone so discreet about the likes of Mrs John Dashwood and Lucy Steele, Elinor is remarkably frank about Marianne's flaws: "Her systems have all the unfortunate tendency of setting propriety at nought; and a better acquaintance with the world is what I look forward to as her greatest possible advantage" (56).

Elinor insists to Colonel Brandon that Marianne is still excusing Willoughby: "I have been more pained ... by her endeavours to acquit him than by all the rest" (211), even when this does not appear to be the case. In fact, if anyone is prone to make excuses, it is Elinor, who is "consoled by the belief that Edward had done nothing to forfeit her esteem" (141). The similarities between Edward's and Willoughby's conduct are striking, and it takes all of Elinor's resources to rationalize them away. Again and again we see her engage in the same behaviour that she criticizes in Marianne. When she sees "a plait of hair" (98) in Edward's ring, Elinor "instantaneously felt" that "the hair was her own": she "was conscious [it] must have been procured by some theft or contrivance unknown to herself" (98). Similarly, Elinor interprets Edward's "want of spirits, of openness, and of consistency" in a way that is consistent with her own desire: "It was happy for her that he had a mother whose character was so imperfectly known to her, as to be the general excuse for every thing strange on the part of her son" (101).

It is the novel's triumph that it keeps hinting at the "other" side, a liberality extended even to the villains. From Elinor's perspective, poor Edward was trapped by the scheming Lucy; clearly, Marianne is not the only quixotic character: the young man seduced by the money-hungry schemer is one of the oldest stories in the book and one that Elinor has to believe. But, as Johnson reminds us, Edward "forms an early attachment out of the idleness endemic to landed gentlemen" (1988, 56) and Lucy is one of his victims. Elinor's conflicted emotions about Willoughby are another case in point, and indeed, many readers cannot help but have some sympathy for Willoughby. And however culpable he is in his treatment of the second Eliza, he also is right in questioning the objectivity of Colonel Brandon's narration: "I do not mean to justify myself, but at the same time cannot leave you to suppose that I have nothing to urge – that because she was injured she was irreproachable, and because I was a libertine, *she* must be a saint" (Austen 1988, 1:322).

Throughout, the novel's project is to point out that nature is carefully wrought artifice. The Palmers' Cleveland gardens may flaunt their artistry with Grecian temples, and Edward may tease

Marianne's interest in books that "tell ... her how to admire an old twisted tree" (92), but the utilitarian "pleasure" that he finds in "a snug farmhouse ... and a troop of tidy, happy villagers" (98) is hardly more natural. In *Sense and Sensibility*, equally "natural" possibilities intersect. Elinor's opinions are juxtaposed to Marianne's and both think they are right: "Such behaviour as this, so exactly the reverse of her own, appeared no more meritorious to Marianne than her own had seemed faulty" to Elinor (104). That is, of course, until the conversion. The underdeveloped character of the third sister, Margaret, further illustrates the novel's point. In the story of war between sense and sensibility, there is no room for a third. By the end of the novel, there is no room even for one "other" sister, as all difference has been neutralized into a harmonious melting pot: "There was that constant communication which strong family affection would naturally dictate ... they could live without disagreement between themselves, or producing coolness between their husbands" (380). The way of achieving this harmony, however, has been less than peaceful. Marvin Mudrick's provocative reading is partly right: the story *is* "tidied up into its prudent conclusion," but not because Jane Austen is an emotionally stunted author who uses irony as "a defense against feeling" (1952, 85). Marianne is indeed "burie[d] in the coffin of convention" (91), but the text exposes this burial – not because it is an early, clumsy work that failed to "pull off" its didactic message but because the text places this process of coercion in the foreground, rather than naturalizing it.

The success of the 1995 film version will do much to enhance the status of *Sense and Sensibility*, and the film is refreshing in its unapologetic celebration of the novel. On the other hand, it corrects precisely those areas that critics have identified as the novel's weaknesses. Edward's personality and honesty are greatly improved (as are his looks); he attempts to tell Elinor about his engagement and it is the evil sister that prevents the disclosure. Elinor's sense does steer her in the right direction, whereas Marianne has to become more like her sister; the film thus presents a didactic reading of the novel. Moreover, Marianne appears to learn her lesson quite happily. The film gives us moving scenes of Marianne falling in love with a Colonel Brandon who is as full of passion as Willoughby. He too can read with great feeling and Emma Thompson's screenplay invents a dramatic second rescue: carrying Marianne in his arms out of the storming rain, Colonel Brandon looks like "Willoughby's ghost" (Thompson 1995, 179). The film reassures us that "there is nothing lost, but may be found, if sought" (187). In order not to disrupt this narrative, Willoughby's confession had to be cut. Thompson admits that "bringing Willoughby back at the end" is a "wonderful scene in the novel," but it "unfortunately interfered too much with the Brandon love story" (272). Naturalizing what the novel denaturalizes, the film tells a great love story, but it is not Jane Austen's.[2]

Austen's dialogic novel does not side with Elinor, or even with Marianne. Instead, it investigates the struggle between them and the process of achieving ideological dominance. *Sense and Sensibility*'s two heroines, at odds for much of the novel, allow us to recognize a pattern in *Emma, Mansfield Park*, and *Persuasion*.

2 See Troost and Greenfield, eds., *Jane Austen in Hollywood* for a collection of essays on film and television adaptations.

CHAPTER TWO

"Exactly the something which her home required":
The "unmerited punishment" of Harriet Smith in Emma

~

Harriet Smith appears in Highbury for the purpose of education at Mrs Goddard's school, "where girls might be sent to be out of the way and scramble themselves into a little education, without any danger of coming back prodigies" (Austen 1988, 4:22). Clearly, Emma is not the only one coming of age in this *Bildungsroman*. Harriet, however, becomes recruited for Emma's process of education within a quixotic narrative that centres on Emma. This narrative (both in the novel and in criticism) is a monologic one. However, Austen incorporates problems that the main narrative cannot come to terms with and must forcibly exclude, namely, Harriet Smith; Austen thereby challenges the completeness of a monologic design with polyphonic otherness.

Emma has often been seen as a female Quixote who patterns real life on the romance genre. According to Walton Litz, the "basic movement in *Emma* is from delusion to self-recognition, from illusion to reality" (1965, 133). For Marilyn Butler, "the theme … is the struggle towards a fixed and permanent truth external to the individual; and chastening, necessarily, of individual presumption and self-consequence" (1987, 260). Duckworth similarly argues that "a central concern of the novel" is "the essentially limited nature of individual human perception" (1994, 162). Crucial to the taming of Emma's imagination is the figure of Harriet, who, both "imagined" and "real," becomes the site for Emma's education process.

"The natural daughter of somebody" (Austen 1988, 4:22), Harriet Smith is in a precarious social position typical of eighteenth-century heroes and heroines, such as Henry Fielding's Tom Jones and Frances Burney's Evelina. The young Austen mocks this tradition in the history of Philander and Gustavus in "Love and Freindship":

We are the sons as you already know, of the two youngest Daughters which Lord St Clair had by Laurina an Italian opera girl. Our mothers could neither of them exactly ascertain who were our fathers; though it is generally beleived [*sic*] that Philander, is the son of one Philip Jones a Bricklayer and that my father was Gregory Staves a Staymaker of Edinburgh. This is however of little consequence, for as our Mothers were certainly never married to either of them, it reflects no Dishonour on our Blood, which is of a most ancient & unpolluted kind. (1988, 6:106–7)

Emma too is convinced that Harriet will "no doubt" prove to be "a gentleman's daughter" (1988, 4:30).

Harriet, one of the many girls at Mrs Goddard's school, is chosen to be Emma's friend. Emma "had long felt an interest in [her], on account of her beauty" (22), but what makes Harriet, as opposed to the also beautifully poor Jane Fairfax, especially interesting to Emma is her "shewing so proper and becoming a deference, seeming so pleasantly grateful for being admitted to Hartfield, and so artlessly impressed by the appearance of every thing in so superior a style to what she had been used to" (23). Emma decides that Harriet "would be a valuable addition," and her "intimacy at Hartfield was soon a settled thing" (26). Harriet's malleability, availability, and utter dependence ("For Mrs Weston there was nothing to be done; for Harriet every thing") make her suitable raw material for Emma and feed Emma's ideas of her own "usefulness" to Harriet (27): "*She* would notice her; she would improve her; she would detach her from her bad acquaintance, and introduce her into good society; she would inform her opinions and her manners" (23–4). Emma wants to mould the "truly artless" Harriet into a heroine (142). We see Emma literally making Harriet over in the portrait scene: "She meant to throw in a little improvement to the figure, to give a little more height, and considerably more elegance" (47). As

Peter Sabor points out, Emma's "plan of making Harriet Smith the subject of whole-length portrait in water-colours ... rais[es] Harriet's value and social standing" (1996, 23–4). Emma's fixation on bringing out the "real" Harriet Smith – the one entitled to position and wealth – is her attempt to be the authority on Harriet and to consume and contain her simultaneously. Harriet becomes Emma's subject, to be painted and sculpted.

Harriet's education is to be subtle so as to give the impression that she is acting out of her own "real" desires and in her own "real" interests. This is the imaginative leap Harriet, and any ideological subject in schooling, is expected to take. Austen, however, makes us see that there is a gap between Harriet's desires and her actions, which is in fact filled in by Emma's desires. The case of Robert Martin provides a good example. In love and wanting to accept his marriage proposal, Harriet is coerced into rejecting him. Although signed by Harriet, the letter of refusal is really Emma's:

Emma assured her there would be no difficulty in the answer, and advised its being written directly ... and though Emma continued to protest against any assistance being wanted, it was in fact given in the formation of every sentence. The looking over his letter again, in replying to it, had such a softening tendency, that it was particularly necessary to brace her up with a few decisive expressions ... This letter, however, was written, and sealed, and sent. The business was finished, and Harriet safe. (Austen 1988, 4:55)

The skill of Emma's manipulation lies in the fact that it seems like Harriet's independent and mature choice to refuse Robert Martin: "Miss Woodhouse, as you will not give me your opinion, I must do as well as I can by myself" (53).

Whether or not Emma's intervention is "a bad thing" (36) is debated between Mr Knightley and Mrs Weston, but it is clear that Harriet is being schooled in the ways of the gentry because of Emma's decisiveness and power to influence. And, of course, it is Emma who receives the credit for Harriet's improvement. Emma is "extremely gratified" (331) when Mr Knightley retracts his former conviction that Harriet is too low for Mr Elton: " 'I will do you the justice to say, that you would have chosen for him better than he has chosen for himself. – Harriet Smith has some first-rate qualities, which Mrs Elton is totally without. An unpretending, single-minded, artless girl – infinitely to be preferred by any man of sense and taste to such a woman as Mrs Elton. I found Harriet more con-versable than I expected' " (ibid.). During the Donwell Abbey visit, we see Knightley and Harriet "in pleasant conversation," for Knightley no longer "scorned her as a companion" (360).

Emma may think Harriet is too good for Robert Martin, but there are limits to Harriet's rise. Harriet is allowed to go only so far. Mr Elton, a "nobody" (136) after all, would never do for Emma: "And he was really a very pleasing young man, a young man whom any woman not fastidious might like" (35). And once Emma de-cides that she does not love Frank Churchill, she graciously passes him over to Harriet, who always takes secondary place to Emma. This is why Harriet is "exactly the something which ... [Emma's] home required" (26). Harriet is used to legitimize Emma's power. More intelligent and decisive than Harriet, Emma "deserves" to have more power, and since she helps her friend along, she may be said to rule benevolently. After all, a Harriet who cannot decide be-tween yellow and blue ribbons at Ford's could not possibly deal with the important decisions that Emma must make. No one (whether in the main quixotic narrative or in most of the criticism, which reproduces this monologic model) acknowledges that Har-riet's indecision is a function of her lack of resources; she cannot decide whether to send the ribbon to Mrs Goddard's or Hartfield because she does not have a permanent home. Instead, Harriet's class disadvantage is erased and naturalized as her weak character.

By the end of this novel of education, Emma comes to believe or learns that her intimacy with Harriet has been a mistake, as have her plans for the social advancement of her "little friend" (482): "Oh! had she never brought Harriet forward! Had she left her where she ought, and where ... [Mr Knightley] had told her she ought! – Had she not, with a folly which no tongue could express, prevented her marrying the unexceptionable young man who would have made her happy and respectable in the line of life to which she ought to belong – all would have been safe; none of this dreadful sequel would have been" (413–14). Emma's rejection of Harriet seems a part of Emma's growth towards maturity. Class prejudice is naturalized as the exercise of a "discriminating" mind. Harriet is not a "gentleman's daughter" after all: "She proved to be the daughter of a tradesman, rich enough to afford her the comfortable maintenance which had ever been her's, and decent enough to have always wished for concealment" (481–2). And just as Emma had imagined Harriet's class position, it becomes clear that she had also imagined her natural worth. In this quixotic narrative, both Harriet's "imagined" and "real" worth are a function of Emma's personal growth; Harriet is consumed within the monologic framework of Emma's development. It is not, however, quixotic to think that Harriet is worthy of Emma, Elton, or Churchill. Rather, it is quixotic to think that Harriet's worth as an "individual" is even an issue here.

Harriet's inferior nature is agreed upon by characters in the novel and critics alike. John Hardy writes that Harriet's "claims exist … only in … [Emma's] imagination" (1984, 84). Marvin Mudrick, in love with Marianne, calling her "the passionate and beautiful girl … winning and lovely" (1952, 81), has no such flattery for Harriet: "the unalterably sheeplike Harriet" (189–90) is merely a "nonentity, will-less comic foil … to Emma's wilfulness" (184). Kenneth Moler, putting *Emma* in the context of the reality/romance debate, argues that Austen allows Emma and the reader "a reality that … includes within itself an imaginatively satisfying element of romance" (1968, 182). Harriet's match with Robert Martin, while "it does not quite conform to the extravagant demands of romance, is nevertheless beyond her reasonable expectations," whereas a match between her and Knightley would have been outlandish: "Not only does the [romance] formula not work here, but the reader – and Emma – breathe a sigh of relief at finding that it does not work. One is made to see that there may be circumstances in which, if love were to conquer all, the result would be anything but fortunate. For there is a vast gap between Harriet and Mr Knightley, not merely in birth and fortune, but in intellect and general habits of mind"(184). Marilyn Butler claims that Harriet "exist[s] for the sake of comparison" (1987, 267); that is, Harriet proves the superiority of "the rightful heroine" (269). These readings fail to consider Harriet in her own right and thus reproduce Emma's own narcissism.

In "Emma Woodhouse and the Charms of the Imagination," Susan Morgan argues that Emma has to learn to "see the boundaries of oneself and the separate life of others" (1975, 36). But this does not result in a limitation of Emma's world: "For Emma, growing up is learning the limits of self. And as her domain shrinks the real world enlarges" (37). Morgan places Jane Fairfax in the position of "the dark, realistic heroine whose history most fulfils Emma's fancies," whom Emma initially "misses" (45) but then gains. Morgan's reading of Jane Fairfax opens the possibility of another heroine, but her reading is based on denying the validity of Harriet Smith as a potential other heroine: "Not only does Emma forfeit the pleasures of friendship with Jane – knowing Harriet is so dull. One need only recall Harriet's trying to choose a ribbon at Ford's or her palpitating surrender of Mr Elton's mementoes to realize how tritely conventional her feelings can be" (ibid.). Trying to elucidate Emma's fault in denying other independent worlds, Morgan repeats that fault herself; for she denies Harriet Smith a story of her own and simply reduces her to a puppet, whose only claim to Emma's friendship is her "inferiority and gratitude [which] ensure her control" (42). There is no doubt, according to Morgan, that Jane is "clearly superior" (36) to Harriet and it is Emma's immaturity that makes her choose Harriet as a companion.

But to focus exclusively on Emma's story and to view Harriet's only as a vehicle for Emma's is to miss half of the story. In this other story we see how the dominant narrative tries to naturalize Harriet's exclusion and to naturalize her inferior class position as her inferior personal worth. We see this because the text admits gaps that the official version of Harriet's departure cannot.

Harriet, like Frankenstein's monster, takes on a life of her own and it is precisely this that the main narrative cannot accommodate. Harriet actually starts to believe Hartfield's equivalent of the

American Dream: "More wonderful things have taken place, there have been matches of greater disparity" (Austen 1988, 4:342). She becomes too much of a gentleman's daughter and has "the presumption to raise her thoughts to Mr Knightley" (414), recognizing his worth before Emma ever does. "How infinitely superior … [Mr Knightley] is to every body else … Mr Frank Churchill, indeed! I do not know who would ever look at him in the company of the other. I hope I have a better taste than to think of Mr Frank Churchill, who is like nobody by his side" (405). When Harriet transgresses the boundaries Emma has set, she is flung back to her starting position. Julia Prewitt Brown claims that "in *Emma* Jane Austen insists on the necessity and finally the benevolence of social cooperation: because it alone protects the Harriets and the Miss Bateses of the world, cares for, tolerates, and loves them" (1979, 125). Mr Knightley may rescue Harriet from social humiliation and dance with her at a ball, but this is only a dance around the real issue of Harriet's lack of power. At the end of the novel, we find her where she could have been at the beginning – married to Robert Martin and excluded from Hartfield.

In his chapter "*Emma* and the Dangers of Individualism," Alistair Duckworth argues that at the end of the novel "the social gaps which individual actions threatened to widen, will be closed around the marriage of the central figures" (1994, 176). Referring to Emma's statement that "it would be a great pleasure to know Robert Martin" (Austen 1988, 4:475), Duckworth assures us that "Emma and Knightley will remain the friends of the Martins" (176). This is a complete misreading. If it is a pleasure to know Mr Martin "now," it is only because he takes Harriet off Emma's hands for a seemingly natural reason rather than for the ideological "house-cleaning" of Hartfield. In order to read the novel as a call by the conservative Austen for the regeneration of societal institutions through individual commitment, Duckworth needs to insist on the continued friendship between the Knightleys and Martins. Clearly, this is wishful thinking. Emma and Harriet do not stay friends: "Harriet, necessarily drawn away by her engagements with the Martins, was less and less at Hartfield; which was not to be regretted. – The intimacy between her and Emma must sink; their

friendship must change into a calmer sort of goodwill; and, fortunately, what ought to be, and must be, seemed already beginning,
and in the most gradual, natural manner" (Austen 1988, 4:482).

The social gaps are not bridged; they become further entrenched not only in terms of the actual separation of Emma and
Harriet but even more so because of the attempt to naturalize class
boundaries: "What … must be, seemed already beginning, and in
the most gradual, natural manner." We never see the conversation
in which Emma informs Harriet of her engagement to Knightley.
Harriet is swept away to London under the pretence of a hurt
tooth. Harriet, Austen writes, "was safe in Brunswick Square"
(451). And once married to Martin, she is "retired enough for
safety" (482). Harriet is an embarrassment that has to be swept
away so as not to "stain" (482) the happy union of Knightley and
Emma:

Every blessing of her own seemed to involve and advance the sufferings of
her friend, who must now be even excluded from Hartfield. The delightful
family-party which Emma was securing for herself, poor Harriet must, in
mere charitable caution, be kept at a distance from. She would be a loser in
every way. Emma could not deplore her future absence as any deduction
from her own enjoyment. In such a party, Harriet would be rather a dead
weight than otherwise; but for the poor girl herself, it seemed a peculiarly
cruel necessity that was to be placing her in such a state of unmerited punishment. (450)

The harmony of the social order depends on Harriet's "unmerited
punishment" of exclusion. No longer containable in the quixotic
narrative, she is exiled to the periphery of Highbury. And it is this
process of smothering the "other" heroine for the sake of monologic oneness that we witness in *Emma*.

When Harriet decides to put Elton behind her once and for all,
she says to Emma:

"To convince you that I have been speaking truth, I am now going to
destroy – what I ought to have destroyed long ago – what I ought never to
have kept – I know that very well … However, now I will destroy it all – and it

is my particular wish to do it in your presence, that you may see how rational I am grown ... I cannot call them gifts; but they are things that I have valued very much." She held the parcel towards her, and Emma read the words *most precious treasures* on top. (337–8)

The treasures are a bit of leftover pencil and plaister, and to Emma they are a source of amusement, revealing Harriet's naïvety; Emma's "feeling[s were] divided between wonder and amusement. And secretly she added to herself, 'Lord bless me ... I never was equal to this'" (339). Emma suggests keeping the plaister, thus denying its emotional significance to Harriet, but Harriet insists that she "shall be happier to burn it ... It has a disagreeable look to me" (340). The point is that what looks ridiculous to Emma is indeed "precious" from Harriet's point of view. Given Emma's class position, these "treasures" look vastly inferior to her idea of a proper love token, a portrait that signals wealth and class position. The idea of something meaning a great deal to one person and nothing to someone else is emblematic of polyphony and it is crucial that Austen allows us to see what is precious to Harriet, not just to Emma; like Mr Watts in Austen's juvenile story "The Three Sisters," Emma has "no idea of any other person's liking" what she "hates" (Austen 1988, 6:58). The novel's dialogism transcends this narcissism. Harriet's final exclusion from Hartfield, like Mary Crawford's from Mansfield Park, draws attention to the inability of the main narrative to account for all.

CHAPTER THREE

"A corrupted, vitiated mind":
The Decline of Mary Crawford in Mansfield Park

~

Mansfield Park, Jane Austen's least-popular novel, has been a particular target of polemical interpretation. For Ian Watt, the novel is "straight-forward" in its "didacticism" (1963, 13). According to Lionel Trilling, its "praise is not for social freedom but for social stasis" and it "takes full notice of spiritedness, vivacity, celerity, and lightness, but only to reject them" (1955, 211). Similarly, Tony Tanner asserts that "*Mansfield Park* is a stoic book in that it speaks for stillness rather than movement, firmness rather than fluidity, arrest rather than change, endurance rather than adventure" (1986, 173). At its centre is Fanny Price, sometimes interpreted as the heroine who was not; Marilyn Butler writes that "to some extent Fanny's is a negation of what is commonly meant by character" (1987, 247). In political interpretations, her stoic resistance to change represents anti-Jacobin resistance to Jacobinism. The novel's ending is then read as the triumph of conservatism over radicalism: Fanny is rewarded, while the Crawfords and anyone connected to them are expelled. According to Butler, Fanny belongs to the heroines who are "right," who embody the conservative case and bring about the education of someone else. In order for the happy end to occur, it is Edmund who has to relearn his values. Fanny's opinions never change, and although she puts Edmund in the position of the lover-mentor, it is really Edmund who has to grow up. His love for Mary Crawford is a moral failure. Mary Crawford is put in the category of the undesirable whose dangerous appeal must be resisted. But the text is much more ambiguous towards Mary Crawford than this (monologic) reading implies.

Mary Crawford arrives at the Mansfield parsonage to visit her sister, Mrs Grant. Initially, Mary is set up as a character in a *Bildungsreise*. Mrs Grant feels confident that "Mansfield shall cure" her (Austen 1988, 3:47). But rather than her learning the error of her ways, her "flaws" become more pronounced: Mary's sin is speaking as "she ought not to" (63). Her speech is characterized by irreverence and often accompanied by her "laughing" (86, 108). As Edmund puts it, "Your lively mind can hardly be serious even on serious subjects" (87). Laughter, as Bakhtin emphasizes, "demolishes fear and piety before an object, before a world, making of it an object of familiar contact and thus clearing the ground for an absolutely free investigation of it" (1981, 23), thus challenging monologic authority. In her "free investigations," Mary insists on privileging her personal experience. Throughout the novel, we see her taking liberties with the Church, the navy, and Mansfield Park, the very institutions that are held in "fear and piety" by Fanny.

Mary refers to the admiral, her "honoured uncle," as "not the first favourite in the world" (Austen 1988, 3:57) and bluntly states that she has been "little addicted to take my opinions from my uncle" (111). Similarly, his profession "is not a favourite ... of mine. It has never worn an amiable form to *me*." Mary has much to say "of various admirals ... of them and their flags, and the gradation of their pay, and their bickerings and jealousies ... my home at my uncle's brought me acquainted with a circle of admirals. Of *Rears* and *Vices*, I saw enough. Now, do not be suspecting me of a pun, I entreat'" (60). Mary's famous "salacious pun" (Johnson 1988, 111) has often been quoted as evidence of Mary's irreverence in opposition to the solemnity of Fanny and Edmund, who "felt grave, and only replied, 'It is a noble profession'" (60). Alice Chandler reads Mary's sexual pun as evidence that Austen "was rather more knowing than has been realized" (1975, 91).

Mary's opinions about the Church are also formed by her personal experience: "I am not entirely without the means of seeing what clergymen are, being at this present time the guest of my own brother Dr Grant" (Austen 1988, 3:111). She describes Dr Grant as an "an indolent selfish bon vivant, who must have his palate consulted in every thing, who will not stir a finger for the convenience of any one, and who, moreover, if the cook makes a blunder, is out of humour with his excellent wife" (ibid.). In the case of both the admiral and the doctor, Mary undermines their "noble profession" by emphasizing the primacy to each of bodily gratification; her view of solemnity is always carnivalesque. While Fanny laments the absence of family assembly, for there is "something in a chapel and chaplain so much in character with a great house, with one's ideas of what such a household should be" (86), Mary laughs at this "fine" custom: "It must do the heads of the family a great deal of good to force all the poor housemaids and footmen to leave business and pleasure, and say their prayers here twice a day, while they are inventing excuses themselves for staying away" (86–7). She thinks the "obligation of attendance, the formality, the restraint, the length of time ... a formidable thing, and what nobody likes." If everyone who "used to kneel and gape in that gallery could have foreseen that the time would ever come when men and women might lie another ten minutes in bed, when they woke with a headach, without danger of reprobation, because chapel was missed, they would have jumped with joy and envy" (87). Mary sees the coercive nature of institutions. Church is attended because of "danger of reprobation."

Edmund is nervous about Mary's "speak[ing] so freely," which "did not suit his sense of propriety" (57). As Claudia Johnson points out, "Tacitly courting Mary himself, Edmund is uneasy about a prospective wife's propensity to talk without inhibition ... A man's bad character should stay behind closed doors" (1988, 111). Mary Crawford is not a subscriber to blind family "loyalty." She is outspoken about what she perceives as the mistreatment of her sister and aunt by their respective spouses, Dr Grant and the admiral, "a man of vicious conduct" (Austen 1988, 3:41). She frankly admits that her "poor aunt had certainly little cause to love the state" of matrimony (46), and she pities her "poor sister" who is "forced to stay and bear" Dr Grant, when he is "out of humour" (111). Mary is never guilty of the sins of Maria and Julia Bertram in *Mansfield Park* or Lydia Bennett in *Pride and Prejudice,* and her punishment seems disproportionate; even Lydia Bennett, after all, dines at Longbourn and at Pemberley, while Mary, as we shall see, is exiled forever. Mary's speech ultimately makes her too dangerous for Mansfield Park. Given what she says about the admiral and Dr Grant, what would she say about Mansfield Park? We get some indication that Mansfield Park would not escape unscathed. Mary cannot help but remark that Maria's marriage and Edmund's taking orders upon Sir Thomas's return from Antigua "does put me in mind of some of the old heathen heroes, who after performing great exploits in a foreign land, offered sacrifices to the gods on their safe return" (108). Putting Sir Thomas in the light of a "heathen hero," Mary implies that his imperial activity is unchristian and requires "sacrifices" as appeasement. She turns the dignified Sir Thomas's return into a "parody": "Blest Knight! whose dictatorial looks dispense / To Children affluence, to Rushworth sense" (161).

Even if Edmund "do[es] not censure her *opinions*" about her uncle, he feels that "there certainly *is* impropriety in making them public" (63). In distinguishing between private and public, Edmund resembles Elinor in *Sense and Sensibility*:

"But I thought it was right, Elinor," said Marianne, "to be guided wholly by the opinion of other people. I thought our judgments were given us merely to be subservient to those of our neighbours. This has always been your doctrine, I am sure."

"No, Marianne, never. My doctrine has never aimed at the subjection of the understanding. All I have ever attempted to influence has been the behaviour. You must not confound my meaning." (93–4)

While both Edmund and Elinor are governed by respect for the community and its institutions, Marianne and Mary privilege their own judgments. This is often interpreted as selfishness and indulgence, and at times it may well be. After all, not all of Mary's actions are rooted in "really good feelings" – they "almost purely govern" her (147). But Austen does present Mary's independence in positive contexts. When Mrs Norris tries to coerce Fanny to participate in the play by reminding her yet again that she "shall think her a very obstinate, ungrateful girl, if she does not do what her aunt and cousins wish her – very ungrateful indeed, considering who and what she is," Mary Crawford,

looking for a moment with astonished eyes at Mrs Norris, and then at Fanny, whose tears were beginning to show themselves, immediately said with some keenness, "I do not like my situation; this *place* is too hot for me" – and moved away her chair to the opposite side of the table close to Fanny, saying to her in a kind low whisper as she placed herself, "Never mind, my dear Miss Price – this is a cross evening, – everybody is cross and teasing – but do not let us mind them;" and with pointed attention continued to talk to her and endeavour to raise her spirits, in spite of being out of spirits herself. – By a look at her brother, she prevented any farther entreaty from the theatrical board. (147)

Mary Crawford realizes Fanny is mistreated, openly takes her side, and attempts to comfort her "in spite of being out of spirits herself." This scene is very similar to one in *Sense and Sensibility* in which Marianne "could not bear ... ill-timed praise of another, at Elinor's expense" and she was "provoked ... to say with warmth":

"This is admiration of a very particular kind! – what is Miss Morton to us? – who knows, or who cares, for her? – it is Elinor of whom we think and speak."
 And so saying, she took the screens out of her sister-in-law's hands to admire them herself as they ought to be admired ... urged by a strong impulse of affectionate sensibility, she moved, after a moment to her sister's chair, and putting one arm round her neck, and one cheek close to her's, said in a low, but eager, voice: "Dear, dear Elinor, don't mind them. Don't let them make *you* unhappy." (235–6)

The comparison between Marianne Dashwood and Mary Crawford is a fruitful one, for it invites the questioning of their different fates: *Sense and Sensibility* makes room for Marianne, while *Mansfield Park* exiles Mary.
 Mary Crawford could easily be one of those heroines whose spirit and irreverence are tamed; after all, during the first two-thirds of

the novel, Mary's free speech is no more morally reprehensible than Emma Woodhouse's insulting Miss Bates, or Elizabeth Bennett's free discussion of Darcy's character with Wickham. But unlike Marianne Dashwood, Mary is not schooled in and recruited to the dominant value system. Instead, her flaws become more pronounced and untenable. Mary's irreverence turns into immorality and extreme selfishness. In *Sense and Sensibility*, peripheral characters like Lucy Steele and Fanny Dashwood are exaggerated, negative, displaced versions of both sense and sensibility. Elinor and Marianne remain likeable throughout, while Lucy Steele and Fanny Dashwood use sensibility and sense to hide their own selfishness and greed. Mary Crawford, however, does not have such buffers; she herself comes to bear the brunt of the ideological cleansing at Mansfield. Mary's qualities, once positive, become thoroughly negative. Her "lively mind" (64) turns "corrupted, vitiated" (456). Her once "arch smile" (93) turns "saucy" (459) and offends Edmund. Her belief in the "true London maxim, that every thing is to be got with money" (58), which for the most part of the novel is at war with her genuine feelings for Edmund, turns murderous, when she hears that Edmund's older brother Tom "has a bad chance of ultimate recovery" (433) from his illness:

To have such a fine young man cut off in the flower of his days, is most melancholy ... I really am quite agitated on the subject. Fanny, Fanny, I see you smile, and look cunning, but upon my honour, I never bribed a physician in my life. Poor young man! – If he is to die, there will be *two* poor young men less in the world; and with a fearless face and bold voice would I say to any one, that wealth and consequence could fall into no hands more deserving of them. (434)

Mary insists that hoping for Tom Bertram's death and Edmund's consequent rise in fortune is "natural ... philanthropic and virtuous": "I put it to your conscience, whether 'Sir Edmund' would not do more good with all the Bertram property, than any other possible 'Sir'" (ibid.). Finally, it is Mary's cavalier attitude towards Maria's illicit behaviour that damns her: "So voluntarily, so freely, so coolly to canvass it! – No reluctance, no horror, no feminine – shall I say? no modest loathings!" (454–5). By the end of the novel, Mary's faults are irredeemable: hers is "a perversion of mind which made it natural to her to treat the subject [of Maria's adultery] as she did. She was speaking only, as she had been used to hear others speak, as she imagined every body else would speak" (456). She is a chilling example of "what the world does" (455) and she must be removed from sight, for she, like Maria Bertram, is "an insult to the neighbourhood" (465). Rejected by Edmund, Mary Crawford takes up residence in London with Mrs Grant.

As D.A. Miller points out, "In the last hundred or so pages of *Mansfield Park*, Mary Crawford disappears from direct view." Mary, the dissipated opportunist, "is represented only by her letters to Fanny and by Edmund's report of his last meeting with her" (1981, 83). In order to provide ideological closure, Edmund and Fanny have to be right and Mary horribly wrong. Mary's voice needs to be taken away so that everyone speaks the same language at home.

Fanny and Edmund's marriage can never be free of the shadow of Mary. Their union is undercut by its very constructedness, which robs it of its power to naturalize the Jacobin ideology; as Claudia Johnson points out, Austen "calls attention to the parodic elements of her denouement" (1988, 114). Fanny's happy ending is deliberately undercut:

I purposely abstain from dates on this occasion, that every one may be at liberty to fix their own, aware that the cure of unconquerable passions, and the transfer of unchanging attachments, must vary much as to time in different people. – I only intreat every body to believe that exactly at the time when it was quite natural that it should be so, and not a week earlier, Edmund did cease to care about Miss Crawford, and became as anxious to marry Fanny, as Fanny herself could desire. (470)

Austen draws attention to the paradoxes underlying the union: the "cure of unconquerable passions" and the "transfer of unchanging attachments." The discourse that approves of the marriage between Fanny and Edmund is counterpointed by the scepticism implicit in the parodying discourse. That Edmund did "care about Miss Craw-ford" cannot be written out of the closure of the novel. Through-out the novel, Mary and Fanny compete for centrality and Fanny's victory is shown to be highly provisional. Fanny's position is further challenged by the newcomer Susan, who "succeeded so naturally to her [Fanny's] influence over the hourly comfort of her aunt, as gradually to become, perhaps, the most beloved of the two" (472–3). At the very end, the ironic and irreverent voice that we have come to associate with Mary Crawford re-enters the narrative and desanctifies the novel's last glance at Mansfield Park.

CHAPTER FOUR

"You are never sure of a good impression being durable":
The Fall of Louisa Musgrove in Persuasion

∾

Louisa Musgrove has never been a favourite with the critics. She is often invoked to prove the superiority of Anne; Louisa is the obstacle between Captain Wentworth and Anne; she is Wentworth's mistake to which the forgiving main narrative fortunately does not hold him. While Anne knows her feelings throughout, Wentworth undergoes the evolution of feeling characteristic of heroines like Elizabeth Bennett and Emma Woodhouse. Louisa is turned into a tool that marks the growth of Wentworth. Alistair Duckworth argues that Wentworth "takes the spoiled wilfulness of Louisa for genuine fortitude" and he "must come to see that it is Anne who possesses true strength of mind" (1994, 197). Similarly, Marilyn Butler states that "the meaning of the accident on the Cobb – that Anne is strong while Louisa is only childishly wilful – is directed at the moral understanding of Captain Wentworth and of the reader" (1987, 279). The accident at Lyme knocks poor Louisa senseless but brings Wentworth to his senses: "Till that day, till the leisure for reflection which followed it, he had not understood the perfect excellence of the mind with which Louisa's could so ill bear a comparison; or the perfect, unrivalled hold it possessed over his own. There, he had learnt to distinguish between the steadiness of principle and the obstinacy of self-will, between the darings of heedlessness and the resolution of a collected mind" (Austen 1988, 5:242). In the words of John Wiltshire, "Narratively, Louisa's tumble is no accident" (1992, 6).

After the fall, Louisa almost disappears from the narrative. She never appears directly, and when we hear of her, she is engaged to Colonel Benwick and described as "altered" by Charles Musgrove:

"There is no running or jumping about, no laughing or dancing; it is quite different. If one happens only to shut the door a little hard, she starts and wriggles like a young dab chick in the water; and Benwick sits at her elbow, reading verses, or whispering to her, all day long" (Austen 1988, 5:218).

She is similar to Marianne Dashwood, who also undergoes physical trauma and wakes up as a new woman in order to accommodate the main narrative. Louisa receives rather cruel punishment; she ends up as the very opposite of the "beautiful glossy nut, which, blessed with original strength, has outlived all the storms of autumn" to which Wentworth compared her: she becomes like "so many of its brethren [which] have fallen and been trodden under foot" (88).

From Louisa's perspective, Wentworth is hardly the honourable hero, and her story very much threatens the narrative of Wentworth and Anne.[1] Wentworth claims that he never cared for Louisa, that in fact she was a mistake: "In his preceding attempts to attach himself to Louisa Musgrove (the attempts of angry pride), he protested that he had forever felt it to be impossible; that he had not cared, could not care for Louisa" (242). He claims that Louisa's affections became involved without any conscious intentions on his part: " 'I found,' said he, 'that I was considered by Harville an engaged man! ... I was startled and shocked. To a degree, I could contradict this instantly; but, when I began to reflect that others might have felt the same – her own family, nay, perhaps herself, I was no longer at my own disposal. I was hers in honour if she wished it. I had been unguarded. I had not thought seriously on this subject before' " (242). He had "entangled" himself and "it determined him to leave Lyme and await her complete recovery elsewhere. He would gladly weaken, by any fair means, whatever feelings or speculations concerning him might exist" (243).

---

1 In "'Unvarying, warm admiration every where': The Truths about Wentworth" (1994), Kathleen James-Cavan and I present a conversation between Anne (Elliot) Wentworth and Louisa (Musgrove) Benwick. In this dialogue, their necessarily different constructions of Wentworth come face to face.

Wentworth's rewriting of the relationship with Louisa is not quite in accord with his behaviour towards Louisa prior to the fall that the novel documents. He may claim to be "startled and shocked" to find himself "considered … an engaged man," but the reader is not. Like *Sense and Sensibility*'s Willoughby and Edward Ferrars, Wentworth raises false expectations of engagement; the Austen heroes – Mr Darcy, Mr Knightley, Henry Tilney in *Northanger Abbey*, and Edmund Bertram – on the other hand, are all forthcoming about their intentions. Louisa is very much like the other women characters in Austen whom we see unfairly treated and deceived by dubious male characters. When Anne learns of the marriage of Benwick and Louisa, she worries about how Captain Wentworth might take it: "Perhaps he had quitted the field, had given Louisa up, had ceased to love, had found he did not love her. She could not endure the idea of treachery or levity, or any thing akin to ill-usage between him and his friend. She could not endure that such a friendship as theirs should be severed unfairly" (166). Although Anne is specifically talking about Wentworth and Benwick, the fears apply equally to Wentworth and Louisa's relationship; Anne wilfully blocks out any evidence of "ill-usage." Indeed, the main narrative depends on this process of exclusion.

Once Louisa falls, her perspective is forcibly removed from the novel to facilitate the necessary rewriting of the rise of Wentworth and Anne. Not one to sympathize with Louisa, Susan Morgan describes her fall on the Cobb as "a moment of burlesque reminiscent of the comedy of the Juvenilia": readers "may join in the pleasure of those who were collected on the Cobb 'to enjoy the sight of a dead young lady, nay, two dead young ladies, for it proved twice as fine as the first report'" (1980, 181). The acting out of the trope of the fall draws attention to the exclusion necessary to establish closure. The fall clearly demonstrates that Anne's narrative ascendancy is based on Louisa's descent. Louisa is silenced, literally rendered speechless, allowing Anne to become central and "so proper, so capable" (Austen 1988, 5:114).

Louisa is *Persuasion*'s other heroine, who competes for Wentworth and centrality until she is excluded to facilitate closure.

Austen draws attention to the suppression of her voice, thereby destabilizing the main narrative. This dialogic process is at work in *Sense and Sensibility, Emma,* and *Mansfield Park,* and it culminates in *Persuasion,* in which the other heroine is forcibly dropped from the Cobb and the narrative action.

CHAPTER FIVE

"An itch for acting":
Playing with Polyphony in Mansfield Park

∾

When Mr Yates arrives at Mansfield, he brings with him an "infection" (184) that spreads quickly: "Happily for him, a love of the theatre is so general, an itch for acting so strong among young people, that he could hardly out-talk the interest of his hearers" (121–2). Austen herself enjoyed and participated in theatricals at the Steventon home (William and Richard Austen-Leigh's 1913 *Family Record* documents this activity), but in *Mansfield Park* theatricals bring about a moral crisis. Edmund insists that it would be "very wrong" to stage a play: "In a *general* light, private theatricals are open to some objections, but as *we* are circumstanced, I think it would be highly injudicious, and more than injudicious, to attempt any thing of the kind" (125).

The circumstances of Sir Thomas's absence and Maria's engagement make the "darling project" (158) an improper one to begin with, but the choice of the play makes matters even worse. Tom assures his brother Edmund that they "may be trusted ... in choosing some play most perfectly unexceptionable" (125–6) and that there is no "harm or danger ... in conversing in the elegant written language of some respectable author" (126). But the chosen play is the hardly "unexceptionable" *Lovers' Vows* (1798), Elizabeth Inchbald's adaptation of August von Kotzebue's *Das Kind der Liebe* (1791). Fanny "could hardly suppose her cousins could be aware of what they were engaging in" (137), and even Maria "blushed in spite of herself" (139).

Austen assumes the reader's familiarity with *Lovers' Vows*. Kotzebue was very popular in Austen's day; as L.F. Thompson points out, from 1798 to about 1810, "his name was a household word ... and his plays ... were represented not only in London season after season but on the boards of every market town that could boast such an ornament" (in Kirkham 1983, 93). *Lovers' Vows* ran for forty-two nights in London, and from 1801 to 1805, when Austen was in Bath, there were six performances at the Theatre Royal. Austen may have seen a production of the play during her stay in Bath, and we know that she saw an adaptation of Kotzebue's *Die Versöhnung* (Thomas Dibdin's *The Birthday*) in 1799.

In her preface to *Lovers' Vows*, Elizabeth Inchbald states that her play is more than "mere verbal translation" (in Austen 1988, 3:476) and that she sought to translate the German spirit into the English one, especially in her presentation of Amelia, who "in the original, would have been revolting to an English audience": she tried "to attach the attention and sympathy of the audience by whimsical insinuations, rather than coarse abruptness – the same woman, I conceive, whom the author drew, with the self-same sentiments, but with manners adapted to the English rather than the German taste" (478). Despite this adaptation, the play was nevertheless considered foreign and dangerous in its day. *Lovers' Vows* was repeatedly condemned in the *Anti-jacobin Review, or Weekly Examiner* for its revolutionary implications. A review in *The Porcupine* (7 September 1801) vehemently objects to the play's failure to "excite, in the minds of ... auditors, respect, admiration, and love of our laws, our magistrate, and our religion." The review closes with a patriotic flourish: "We have been free in our animadversions on this exotic production; and we trust that we shall always possess sufficient firmness to oppose, with energy, whatever appears to violate the principles of correct taste, or to militate against political or moral propriety" (in Reitzel 1933, 453).

The exoticizing of the play serves the interest of containment, for its subversive ideas are represented as foreign, as the "objectionable dramas of German notoriety." According to *The Porcupine*, "it is the universal aim of German authors ... to exhibit the brightest examples of virtue among the lower classes of society; while the higher orders, by their folly and profligacy, are held up to contempt and detestation. This is fully exemplified in *Lovers Vows*." The reviewers "have ever beheld, with regret, the avidity with which imported nonsense is attended to, while the truly admirable productions of native genius are thrown by to moulder on the shelf of forgetfulness" (ibid.). Similarly, in his "Preface to *The Lyrical Ballads*" (1798), William Wordsworth laments that "the invaluable works of our elder writers, I had almost said the works of Shakespeare and Milton, are driven into neglect by frantic novels, *sickly and stupid German Tragedies*, and deluges of idle and extravagant stories in verse" (1988, 284; emphasis added).[1] Wordsworth's worst fears come true in *Mansfield Park*: "All the best plays were run over in vain. Neither *Hamlet*, nor *Macbeth*, nor *Othello* … presented any thing that could satisfy even the tragedians" (Austen 1988, 3:130–1).

Lovers' Vows opens with Agatha in a state of destitution. She is reunited with her son Frederick, to whom she reveals the truth about his father. As a young servant girl, she was seduced by her patroness's son, then thrown out of the house, rejected by her parents, and ignored by her lover who married a woman of high social standing and large fortune. Frederick vows to stand by his mother and goes out to beg for her. He assaults Baron Wildenhaim, who imprisons him. The nobleman turns out to be Frederick's father and the pastor Anhalt secures a reconciliation between Frederick, Baron Wildenhaim, and Agatha. At the same time, Wildenhaim's daughter, Amelia, is in love with Anhalt. Her father wants her to marry the rich philanderer Count Cassell, but Amelia convinces her father that love is more important than wealth and class. The play ends very happily with two weddings: that of Wildenhaim and Agatha, and that of Anhalt and Amelia.

The play deals with issues that were especially explosive during the era of the French Revolution. Both marriages transgress class boundaries. When Baron Wildenhaim initially abandons the servant girl Agatha, his behaviour is shown as unequivocally villainous; by the end of the play, the baron repents and marries Agatha. Rather than shunning the fallen woman, Kotzebue's play includes

---

1 In note twelve on page 493, John O. Hayden identifies the "sickly and stupid German tragedies" as Kotzebue's, as does the note in volume two of *The Norton Anthology of English Literature* (161).

her in the happy ending: "the whole village was witness of Agatha's shame – the whole village must be witness of Agatha's re-
established honour" (Inchbald 1798, in Austen 1988, 3:535). In
the relationship between Amelia and Anhalt the mistakes of the
past are not repeated. To Amelia, "birth and fortune were such
old-fashioned things to me, I cared nothing about either" (522–
3); by the end of the play, the baron agrees: "A man of your principles, at once a teacher and an example of virtue, exalts his rank
in life to level with the noblest family – and I shall be proud to receive you as my son" (535). As Marilyn Butler points out, *Lovers'
Vows* "attacks the conventions by which marriage upholds existing
rank, and exalts instead the liaison based on feeling" (1987, 234).
Furthermore, as Paula Backscheider observes, the play "drama-
tizes the destructive effects of poverty and desperation" (1980,
xviii). And the play also challenges conventional femininity; Amelia rejects her father's choice of a husband and actively pursues
her own desire. In the words of Mary Crawford, "Such a forward
young lady may well frighten the men" (Austen 1988, 3:144).
Amelia certainly seems to have "frighten[ed]" *The Porcupine*, according to which she is "coarse, forward, and disgusting, and we
trust, will never be imitated by the British fair" (in Reitzel 1933,
453).

Lovers' Vows never makes it to actual performance in *Mansfield
Park*, and the eventual closing of the play is often taken as evidence
of the conservative stance of the novel. H. Winifred Husbands
claims that Austen's novel functions "chiefly, if not entirely, as a
protest against the lax morality of *Lovers' Vows*" (1934, 176). Marilyn Butler agrees: "The imagined free world which comes into being on the stage is a comprehensible entity, the clearest image in all
of Jane Austen's novels of what she is opposed to" (1987, 233): "A
sanguine believer in the fundamental goodness and innocence of
human nature, the apostle of intuition over convention, indeed of
sexual liberty over every type of restraint, [Kotzebue] is a one-sided
propagandist for every position which the anti-jacobin novelist ab-
hors" (234). Marc Baer also sees Sir Thomas's opposition to the
play as Jane Austen's: "We should take at face value Sir Thomas
Bertram's/Jane Austen's concerns about the family performing"

Lovers' Vows (1992, 253). Even a critic interested in dialogism takes "Austen's disapproval of her amateur thespians" as a given (Baldridge 1994, 51). The "right" characters are "against" it; the "bad" ones are "for" it; Edmund's participation is a sign of the moral danger to which his love for Mary Crawford exposes him. In "Love and Freindship," the immoral Gustavus and Philander join "some strolling Company of Players, as we had always a turn for the stage" (Austen 1988, 6:107), but *Mansfield Park* does not adopt this moralistic stance towards the theatre.

By allowing *Lovers' Vows*, a play that challenges Mansfield values, into the novel, Austen denics Mansfield control over language. *Lovers' Vows* comes, literally, from a different language, and this language is admitted into the novel. Sir Thomas's desperate attempt to purge it fails. The play cannot be contained and it spills over into the fabric of the novel as a whole.

Lovers' Vows presents a discourse that challenges the value structure embedded in Mansfield. As A. Walton Litz points out, "With its emphasis on feeling and disregard for traditional restraints, with its contempt for social form, *Lovers' Vows* stands as an emblem of those forces which threaten the neoclassical security of Mansfield Park" (1965, 125). When Sir Thomas, upon returning to Mansfield, "found himself on the stage of a theatre, and opposed to a ranting young man, who appeared likely to knock him down backwards" (Austen 1988, 3:182), he is confronted not just with Mr Yates but with an ideology that challenges or "appeared likely to knock ... down" his own. *Lovers' Vows* brings to the surface exactly what Sir Thomas's discourse seeks to repress. The play exposes Baron Wildenhaim's indiscretion; illicit love has no place in Sir Thomas's self-definition as the benevolent patriarch.[2] He reacts by burning

2 Frank Gibbon, in the article that first pointed out the Austen family's connection with the Nibbs family and Antigua, argues that "Jane Austen would certainly have been aware of the likelihood of a family such as her fictional Bertrams having numerous mulatto relatives in Antigua" (1982, 304–5). Moira Ferguson asks in response to Gibbon: "Does Sir Thomas banish his daughter Maria and censure Henry Crawford because their sexual indulgences mirror his Antiguan conduct? Is one dimension of his behavior a form of self-projection, an unconscious denial of his dual and contradictory realities in the Caribbean and Britain?" (1993, 78).

"every unbound copy of *Lovers' Vows*" (191) and when Maria exposes his failure as a patriarch, she too is purged. Maria is not only
an "insult to the neighbourhood" (465) but, more importantly, an
insult to himself. The play questions the trading of one's daughter
to a rich fool, a fault that Sir Thomas is conscious of committing in
his deal with Mr Rushworth: "Such and such-like were the reason-
ings of Sir Thomas – happy to escape the embarrassing evils of a
rupture, the wonder, the reflections, the reproach that must attend
it, happy to secure a marriage which would bring him such an addition of respectability and influence, and very happy to think any
thing of his daughter's disposition that was most favourable for the
purpose" (201). Brought face to face with Baron Wildenhaim, Sir
Thomas is made to look into a mirror and he does not like what he
sees. Sir Thomas's vision of himself is based on partial blindness;
like any ideology, his vision covers up the "real conditions of [his]
existence" (Althusser 1971, 153).

The scene, however, goes significantly beyond the confrontation
in which Sir Thomas's imposing "looks of solemnity and amaze-
ment" bully Mr Yates into a "bow and apology." Tom's presence
and "difficulty in keeping his countenance" (182) desanctify the
confrontation between Sir Thomas and Mr Yates. It too becomes a
play: "It would be the last – in all probability the last scene on that
stage; but he was sure there could not be a finer. The house would
close with the greatest eclat" (182–3). From this angle even
Sir Thomas's discourse is a role. There is nothing essential or
absolute about it; its monologic authority is destroyed and it is
only a part in the play of polyphony. Litz argues that "the ability
'to act a part' becomes a touchstone to insincerity" (1965, 126),
but the fact that the Crawfords, the Bertrams, Mr Rushworth, and
Mr Yates act does not signify their lack of true feeling so much as
the dialogism of the novel. Henry's ability to present several voices
"with equal beauty" resembles the dialogic nature of the novel
itself:

In Mr Crawford's reading there was a variety of excellence beyond what she
had ever met with. The King, the Queen, Buckingham, Wolsey, Cromwell,

all were given in turn; for with the happiest knack, the happiest power of jumping and guessing, he could always light, at will, on the best scene, or the best speeches of each; and whether it were dignity or pride, or tenderness or remorse, or whatever were to be expressed, he could do it with equal beauty. (337)

Even Fanny cannot help but be seduced sometimes:

Edmund watched the progress of her attention, and was amused and gratified by seeing how she gradually slackened in the needle-work, which, at the beginning, seemed to occupy her totally; how it fell from her hand while she sat motionless over it – and at last, how the eyes which had appeared so studiously to avoid him throughout the day, were turned and fixed on Crawford, fixed on him for minutes, fixed on him in short till the attraction drew Crawford's upon her, and the book was closed, and the charm was broken. (337)

And with Edmund watching this scene, it too becomes like a play and Fanny an actor in it.

The play within the novel is emblematic of polyphony. The "other" heroines are avenues into the polyphony of Austen's texts. Elinor Dashwood, Emma Woodhouse, Fanny Price, and Anne Elliot are just actors in a drama that is larger than they are; they have to share the stage with others. *Sense and Sensibility* and *Persuasion* are further dialogized by the interaction between present and past narratives. In both novels and in *Pride and Prejudice*, the past provides a source of tension and disruption of the main narrative. In this way, the function of the "narrative cameo" is similar to that of the "other" heroine.

PART TWO

"Their fates, their fortunes, cannot be the same":
Cameo Appearances

~

How wonderful, how very wonderful the operations of time, and the changes of the human mind! ... If any one faculty of our nature may be called *more* wonderful than the rest, I do think it is memory. There seems something more speakingly incomprehensible in the powers, the failures, the inequalities of memory, than in any other of our intelligences. The memory is sometimes so retentive, so serviceable, so obedient – at others, so bewildered and so weak – and at others again, so tyrannic, so beyond controul! – We are to be sure a miracle every way – but our powers of recollecting and of forgetting, do seem peculiarly past finding out.

(Austen 1988, 3: 208–9)

Sense and Sensibility, Persuasion, and *Pride and Prejudice* incorporate past narratives: the story of the two Elizas, the story of Mrs Smith, and the story of Wickham and Georgiana respectively. In their frankness about financial and sexual exploitation, these stories have been considered as strikingly incongruous and sometimes as awkward anomalies in Austen's fiction. Susan Morgan's *In the Meantime: Character and Perception in Jane Austen's Fiction* (1980) makes the following astute comment on Austen scholarship: "The idea that *Persuasion* is an exception, like the ideas that *Sense and Sensibility* or *Mansfield Park* are exceptions, is based on a view of Austen's work which, finally, is too exclusive" (171). By the same token, an alleged anomaly within an individual novel is the product of the limitations of a critical approach. Morgan herself makes this critical error, when she refers to the embedded narratives in *Persuasion, Sense and Sensibility,* and *Pride and Prejudice* as "uncomfortably conspicuous" (176) and "out of place" (177). The cameos are deliberately in place, and interpretation has to make room for them; after all, Austen's novels do. Rosemary Hennessy, in *Materialist Feminism and the Politics of Discourse* (1993), points out that "symptomatic weaknesses in the coherence of any text are the residues of unanswered questions inscribed in the structuring of the ... discourse, disrupting the preconstructed categories on which it depends. To read a text symptomatically is to make visible that which hegemonic ideology does not mention, those things which must not be spoken, discursive contestations which are naturalized in the ... discourse but which still shape the text's dis-eased relation to itself" (94). To bring the "narrative cameos" to the foreground is, in Hennessy's terms, to read Austen's texts "symptomatically," for the cameos reveal what the dominant ideology represses.

The narrative cameos challenge some common assumptions about Austen. The novels are narrow in their chosen social milieu; yet the cameos deal with illegitimate children, fallen women, and abject poverty. Austen is conservative, for she reconciles the desire of the individual with the structure of society; the cameos show just the opposite: individuals for whom the social order has failed. The cameos provide a countercurrent to the main narrative. They articulate what the main narrative tries to elide and are thus integral to the design of the novels.

These brief narratives destabilize the main narratives and are vehicles of dialogism. In *Sense and Sensibility,* there are distinct parallels between the cameo and the main narrative, but the cameo also mirrors back to the main narrative an inverse image of itself, thereby destabilizing it. In *Persuasion,* the cameo brings to the surface the exploitation that permeates the main narrative and facilitates its resolution. And *Pride and Prejudice*'s tale of Wickham's almost-successful seduction of Georgiana darkens the novel's so-called fairy-tale ending. In all three cases, the cameos point out the extreme precariousness of the novels' endings and provide alternative closures.

Each cameo is, in a sense, the ur-novel that the present narrative rewrites. These three novels start long before the first page, but that beginning is buried until it is resurrected as a memory in the midst of the novel. How do the main narratives accommodate these memories? Does history repeat itself, or is it transformed? The structures of the novels reproduce the act of remembering. These acts of memory are always incomplete and always potentially destructive of the stasis they interrupt. The acts are incomplete in the sense that when the memory is repeated in the present tense, it is transformed into a positive ending that leaves out the material that the present narrative cannot accommodate. In the rewriting of the past, its contradictions are eliminated. Hence, by juxtaposing an ur-version with the present narrative, Austen reveals the construction of ideology in the process. The incorporation of both narratives facilitates dialogism. Part One of this study has examined the voices of the other heroines as vehicles of dialogism. The cameos function in the same manner. Just as Harriet dialogizes Emma's story, the tale of the two Elizas dialogizes that of Marianne Dashwood in *Sense and Sensibility*. That novel, with the accommodation of its two competing heroines, lends itself particularly well to this kind of analysis. Both sense and sensibility are constantly dialogized, and the cameo contributes to this process. Eliza becomes a vehicle of dialogism for Marianne, undermining the closure she reaches. The cameos haunt *Sense and Sensibility, Persuasion,* and *Pride and Prejudice,* pointing out their provisionality, their constructedness, and their precariousness.

CHAPTER SIX

"Surely this comparison must have its use":
The "very strong resemblance" in Sense and Sensibility

∽

In chapter nine of the second volume of *Sense and Sensibility*, Colonel Brandon tells the story of the two Elizas to Elinor. Eliza's guardian, Colonel Brandon's father, disregarded her wishes and, having been "allowed no liberty, no society, no amusement, till ... [his] point was gained" (Austen 1988, 5:206), she was "married against her inclination" to Colonel Brandon's brother: "Her fortune was large, and our family estate much encumbered. And this, I fear, is all that can be said for the conduct of one who was at once her uncle and guardian" (205). Eliza's marriage is described as unhappy: "My brother had no regard for her; his pleasures were not what they ought to have been, and from the first he treated her unkindly" (206). The "misery of her situation" (205) and the "great unkindness" (206) she experienced is repeated twice to emphasize Eliza's "suffering" (207). The narrative then progresses to Eliza's "fall" into "divorce" (206). "Her legal allowance ... not adequate to her fortune, nor sufficient for her comfortable maintenance," she "sink[s] deeper in a life of sin" and "debt," finally dying of "consumption" (207). She leaves her daughter Eliza, "the offspring of her first guilty connection" (208), to the protection of Colonel Brandon. During a stay in Bath, Eliza is seduced by Willoughby and "made poor and miserable" like her mother: "He had left the girl whose youth and innocence he had seduced, in a situation of the utmost distress, with no creditable home, no help, no friends, ignorant of his address! He had left her promising to return; he neither returned, nor wrote, nor relieved her" (209). After the delivery of Eliza's illegitimate child, Brandon "removed her and her child into the country, and there she remains" in exile (211).

Some critics see this passage as a flaw in *Sense and Sensibility*: a degeneration into the gothic or a lack of integration. It is a "hackneyed tale" (Litz 1965, 82) and "uncomfortably conspicuous" (Morgan 1980, 176). Others, such as Claudia Johnson, see the potentially subversive force of the narrative: "Eliza's fate testifies to the failures of conservative ideology" (1988, 56). According to these readings, Austen pushes this potentially subversive material to the margins in order to present an ostensibly conservative narrative; the cameo, therefore, is a strategy of indirection. Johnson argues that although the cameo "is linked to the larger story ... through the use of common thematic and descriptive details" (55–6), it is "never permitted to become central": to have placed the tales of the Elizas in the foreground "would have entailed earmarking a progressive stance, which she [Austen] evidently did not want to do." The narrative is "tuck[ed] ... safely within the centre" of the novel "as if to defuse the sensitivity of the subject matter," and by "delegating its narration to the safe Colonel Brandon," Austen "distance[s] ... herself from the story of the two Elizas" (55). Similarly, according to Mary Poovey, Austen is "so careful ... to keep the reader on the outside of such 'dangerous' material that she embeds the most passionate episodes within other, less emotionally volatile stories" (1984, 187).

The tale of the exploited and fallen women is not, however, confined to the safety of one chapter. The cameo is an integral part of *Sense and Sensibility*, spilling beyond its frame and creating a ripple effect that changes the surface of the novel. The cameo is explicitly alluded to several times during the course of the novel. In chapter 11, Colonel Brandon begins the story but "stopt suddenly" (Austen 1988, 1:57); Elinor retells the story twice to Marianne and to Mrs Dashwood, and she discusses the second Eliza with Willoughby. Describing himself as a "very awkward narrator" (204), Colonel Brandon declares: "A subject such as this – untouched for fourteen years – it is dangerous to handle it at all!" (208). A great deal of anxiety surrounds this narrative precisely because it is not firmly planted in the past.

Nor is Colonel Brandon "safe" (Johnson 1988, 55); for the narrative of the two Elizas could indict him. Colonel Brandon's nervousness is the result not just of pain and delicacy but also of his attempt to cover up his own guilt. When Eliza is married against her will, Brandon is conveniently absent, as he is for all of the second Eliza's misfortunes. He claims that he "gladly would … have discharged" his responsibility towards Eliza "in the strictest sense," but "the nature of our situations" did not "allow" it: "I had no family, no home; and my little Eliza was therefore placed at school." Yet even when "the possession of the family property" provides Colonel Brandon with a home, he "place[s] her under the care of a very respectable woman, residing in Dorsetshire" (Austen 1988, 1:208). Furthermore, Colonel Brandon's reason for not warning the Dashwoods about Willoughby is to protect his own secret rather than Marianne's happiness: "what could I do? I had no hope of interfering with success; and sometimes I thought your sister's influence might yet reclaim him. But now, after such dishonourable usage, who can tell what were his designs on her?" (210). His excuse is perhaps as thin as Willoughby's for abandoning Eliza: "I did not recollect that I had omitted to give her my direction" (322–3). Both Brandon and Willoughby know when to be conveniently absent. The cameo destabilizes the main narrative's construction of Colonel Brandon as the noble and patient hero for whom Marianne "by general consent, was to be the reward" (378).

In the narrative cameo, mother and daughter share the same first name and an "unhappy resemblance" in "fate" (211). Claudia Johnson remarks on the "insistent redundancy" of the tale which "opens the sinister possibility that plights such as theirs proliferate throughout the kingdom" (1988, 57). The narration of the story is sparked by the "very strong resemblance between" Marianne and Eliza "as well in mind as person. The same warmth of heart, the same eagerness of fancy and spirits" (Austen 1988, 1:205). Brandon compares Marianne's looks and temperament to that of the first Eliza, but it is the second Eliza's story that brings home the particular danger Marianne so nearly escaped in her relationship with Willoughby. Marianne shares the second Eliza's love for Willoughby and the consequent betrayal, and she shares the serious illness with the first Eliza: Brandon looks at Marianne during her illness with "the probable recurrence of many past scenes of misery to his mind, brought back by that resemblance between Marianne and Eliza already acknowledged, and now strengthened by the hollow eye, the sickly skin, the posture of reclining weakness" (340). The type of marriage the first Eliza suffers is the one Marianne so closely avoids. Austen emphasizes the similarities between the three women almost to a point of interchangeability. Colonel Brandon insists that "their fates, their fortunes, cannot be the same" (208); that they almost are, however, is the point.

The alignment of Marianne with the two Elizas undermines the narrative closure, for the extreme precariousness of Marianne's "happy ending" is further emphasized. Marianne herself realizes the narrow escape she has made: "She felt the loss of Willoughby's character yet more heavily than she had felt the loss of his heart; his seduction and desertion of Miss Williams, the misery of that poor girl, and the doubt of what his designs might *once* have been on herself, preyed altogether so much on her spirits, that she could not bring herself to speak of what she felt even to Elinor" (212). Marianne's fear of "what his designs might *once* have been on herself" represents the unspeakable, that which the main narrative cannot accommodate. The main narrative elides this unspeakable fate – seduction, pregnancy, prostitution, and exile – and rewrites it into a closure, where the heroine of sensibility "found herself ... submitting to new attachments, entering on new duties, placed in a new home, a wife, the mistress of a family, and the patroness of a village" (379). Marianne wakes up from her illness as the reformed heroine who renounces sensibility and becomes firmly entrenched in a community of sense. The cameo is an insistent reminder of this transformation. It points out literally that the new Marianne is resurrected, and that the two Elizas are her former selves.

Moreover, the cameo narrative serves as a tool to achieve the closure of the main narrative. The tale of the Elizas transforms Colonel Brandon's "forlorn condition as an old bachelor" (37) and reveals him, as Jan Fergus points out, as "a victim of a first attachment" and "a conventional romantic hero" (1983, 53). The tale prepares Marianne for the ascendancy of Brandon. Elinor "saw with satisfaction the effect of it, in her no longer avoiding Colonel Brandon when he called, in her speaking to him, even voluntarily speaking, with a kind of compassionate respect" (Austen 1988, 1:212). At the end of the novel, when we are given the reasons for Marianne's change of heart, one of them is that she had "a knowledge so intimate of his goodness" (378). Colonel Brandon ostensibly tells the story for the didactic purpose of giving "lasting conviction" to Marianne's "mind" (204): "Surely this comparison must have its use with her. She will feel her own sufferings to be nothing" (210).

The story impresses on Marianne the need to restrain sensibility and the need for a male protector, like Colonel Brandon. Yet, as we shall see again in *Mansfield Park*, the medicinal purpose is merely a cloak for coercion. After Elinor carefully repeats it to Marianne, "the conviction of [Willoughby's] guilt *was* carried home to her mind," but, while Elinor "saw her spirits less violently irritated than before, she did not see her less wretched. Her mind did become settled, but it was settled in a gloomy dejection." Although "the effect on … [Marianne] was not entirely such as … [Elinor] had hoped to see," the tale fulfils its brainwashing purpose.[1] It "settle[s]" Marianne into the "dejection" (212) that is necessary to make her "submit" (379) to the "confederacy against her" (378) at the end of the novel. The cameo reveals the violence and coercion that is used to transform Marianne and thereby contributes to the dialogism of the main narrative by revealing how it achieves closure and dominance. The cameo helps to reveal that Marianne's transformation is not so much an educative process in which she learns to see the error of her ways as a process of oppression that forces her to capitulate. The main narrative has to be remarkably brief on the subject of Marianne's change of mind and heart: "But so it was" (378).

---

1 The fact that the "effect" on Marianne is "not entirely such as … [Elinor] had hoped to see" (Austen 1988, 1:212) is significant, for it reveals that Elinor is not fully aware of the nature of Marianne's reformation and her role in it. Elinor's surprise at not seeing Marianne any happier shows that Elinor thinks she is acting out of her sister's best interests throughout.

The cameo in *Sense and Sensibility* bears similarities to main narratives found in other Austen novels. Colonel Brandon's father, who marries off his ward against her inclination, is not very different from *Mansfield Park*'s Sir Thomas. He, after all, attempts to do the same to his ward, Fanny Price; and against his better judgment, he marries his daughter to Mr Rushworth, who is "such an addition of respectability and influence" (ibid., 3:201), with similar results: Maria Bertram elopes and, like Eliza, is exiled to the country. The tyranny of Colonel Brandon's father is also reminiscent of *Northanger Abbey*'s General Tilney. The notion that the cameo is radically different from the rest of Austen is not accurate, and it reflects the limitations that have been imposed on Austen's work by a critical tradition.

CHAPTER SEVEN

"My expressions startle you":
An "injured, angry woman" in Persuasion

~

In chapter nine of the second volume of *Persuasion*, Mrs Smith tells Anne of the ill treatment she and her husband received at the hands of Mr Elliot, "a man without heart or conscience": "Oh! he is black at heart, hollow and black!" (ibid., 5:199). For years Mr Elliot received generous assistance from the Smiths: "He was then the inferior in circumstances, he was then the poor one ... My poor Charles, who had the finest, most generous spirit in the world, would have divided his last farthing with him; and I know that his purse was open to him; I know that he often assisted him" (199–200). The Smiths end in financial "ruin," and before his death, Mr Smith "with a confidence in Mr Elliot's regard ... appointed him executor of his will." Reversal of fortune, however, proved Mr Elliot to be not so kind: he "would not act, and the difficulties and distresses which this refusal had heaped on [Mrs Smith] ... had been such as could not be related without anguish of spirit, or listened to without corresponding indignation." Mr Elliot's "cold civility" and "hard-hearted indifference" (209) paint "a dreadful picture of ingratitude and inhumanity; and Anne felt at some moments, that no flagrant open crime could have been worse" (210). The cameo also alludes to Mr Elliot's first marriage; he had "one object in view – to make his fortune, and by a rather quicker process than the law." His wife, never named in the narrative, dies of a mysterious cause: "they were not a happy couple" (200).

Mrs Smith's narrative sheds light on Mr Elliot's conduct towards the Elliot family. Once "declar[ing], that if baronetcies were saleable, any body should have his for fifty pounds, arms and motto, name and livery included" (202), now "upon all points of blood and connexion, he is a completely altered man" (206): "He cannot

bear the idea of not being Sir William" (207). His ingratiating behaviour towards the Elliots is motivated by a desire to protect his
selfish interest from the aspirations of Mrs Clay, who has her eye on
Sir Walter Elliot's fortune.

This narrative, like its counterpart in *Sense and Sensibility*, has been
considered a weak episode in the novel. Marilyn Butler refers to it as
an "outworn cliché of the eighteenth-century novel ... which Jane
Austen otherwise allows herself only in *Sense and Sensibility*" (1987,
280). As Susan Morgan puts it, Mrs Smith's "dark revelations about
Mr Elliot ... in their conventional indecency, have put off many
readers" (1980, 176). Mrs Smith's "revelation, like Mr Elliot's
wicked character, is a conscious fictional cliché" and "distinctly
gothic" (177), rendering the episode harmless: "The very familiarity
of Mrs Smith's jarring information serves to highlight its
irrelevance ... In *Persuasion* villainy is about as threatening as those
gypsies which pass through Highbury and frighten Harriet Smith"
(176).

Others see a daring quality in the cameo. For Sandra Gilbert and
Susan Gubar, "poor, confined, crippled by rheumatic fever,
Mrs Smith serves as an emblem of the dispossession of women in a
patriarchal society" (1979, 181). Agreeing with Paul Zietlow
(1965), they state that Mrs Smith is "the embodiment of what
Anne's future could have been under less fortunate circumstances"
(ibid.). As John Wiltshire points out, "One function of Mrs Smith is
to anchor the romantic idealism of Anne ... to the grim conditions
of survival": Mrs Smith "restrains the novel's impulse to a day-
dream-like wish-fulfilment (the past restored, the rift healed) by
setting against it a view of life characterized by day-to-day tenacious-
ness and an integrity qualified by necessary expediency" (1992,
181).[1] Wiltshire disagrees with the critical tendency to see

---

1 For Alistair Duckworth, Mrs Smith is one of the novel's examples of "responses to
misfortune" that "define, in both negative and positive ways, the choices open to the de-
prived individual, but they also comment interestingly on Anne's own moral conduct"
(1994, 190). Mrs Smith, he holds, is a negative example. "Mandevillian," "cynical," and
"misanthropic," Mrs Smith's "charity is largely false." Thus, with the aid of her nurse,

Mrs Smith as a "puzzlingly predominant flaw or intrusion" (165) in *Persuasion*: "The extended treatment the figure is given may be seen ... as a crucial elaboration of the thought of the novel ... for the story of Mrs Smith, like the story of Anne Elliot, displays Jane Austen's intense interest in the resources of the human spirit in the face of affliction" (165–6). He insists, however, that this "cannot rescue the melodrama of [Mrs Smith's] unmasking Mr Elliot's 'hollow and black' heart" (166). Wiltshire puts this qualifying phrase in brackets, emphasizing his dismissal of what he also considers "puzzlingly" flawed in *Persuasion*. He argues that Mrs. Smith's "exposure" of Mr Elliot "is, strictly speaking, superfluous since Anne has already made up her own mind not to trust him" (180).

Like the cameo in *Sense and Sensibility*, the story of Mrs Smith points out the precariousness of the heroine's happiness. Although Marilyn Butler contends that Mr Elliot "never represents any kind of real temptation" to Anne (1987, 280), the text itself contradicts this claim: "Anne could just acknowledge within herself such a possibility of having been induced to marry him, as made her shudder at the idea of the misery which must have followed. It was just possible that she might have been persuaded by Lady Russell!" (Austen 1988, 5:211).

Nor can the text get rid of Mr Elliot. Susan Morgan claims that "Austen then disposes of the villain, along with the views of human nature and of literary convention he represents, by banishing him from her novel in company with a freckled villainess" (1980, 177). But this removal is only temporary. Mr Elliot is a permanent

---

"who sells Mrs Smith's products among her rich patients, Mrs Smith is able to obtain (almost to extort) enough money to survive" (192). Referring to Duckworth's statements about Mrs Smith and Nurse Rooke, Wiltshire finds it "amusing to see critics who unquestionably accept the sailors' right to plunder French frigates getting upset at ... [Nurse Rooke and Mrs Smith] taking minor advantage of ... wealthier clients" (1992, 184).
In his introduction to the reprint of *The Improvement of the Estate*, Duckworth retracts his interpretation of Mrs Smith and Nurse Rooke: "Readers should ... be warned not to give too much credit to the interpretation of Mrs Smith on pages 191–2" (1994, xxvii).

member of the Elliot family, firmly entrenched in Sir Walter's baronetage: "Heir presumptive, William Walter Elliot, Esq. great
grandson of the second Sir Walter" (Austen 1988, 5:4). The entry,
ironically, is in Sir Walter's own handwriting and it is safe to assume
that by the end of the novel the baronetage is less of a "consolation
in a distressed" hour (3) for Sir Walter and even more of an "evil"
(7) for Elizabeth. The family relationship marries the cameo and
the main narrative for life.

Furthermore, Mr Elliot's character is hardly so "out of place"
(Morgan 1980, 177) in *Persuasion*: he is "a designing, wary, cold-
blooded being, who thinks only of himself; who, for his own interest or ease, would be guilty of any cruelty, or any treachery, that
could be perpetrated without risk of his general character. He has
no feeling for others" (Austen 1988, 5:199). Mr Elliot's selfishness
is not so different from Sir Walter's or that of Anne's sisters, all of
whom consistently use Anne for their own purposes. The cameo is
a magnifying glass for the novel as a whole. Its look at blatant exploitation dialogizes the novel, for it makes us see what the main
narrative tries to minimize.

Throughout the novel, Anne is exploited at the hands of her family. As John Wiltshire puts it, "the first volume of *Persuasion*, one can
say with only a small exaggeration, is a portrait of suffering" (1992,
155). In many ways the emotional treatment that Anne receives is
similar to that of Fanny Price in *Mansfield Park*. Like Fanny, who is
made to feel like the "lowest and the last" (Austen 1988, 3:221),
Anne is constantly reminded that she "was nobody with either father or sister: her word had no weight; her convenience was always
to give way; – she was only Anne" (ibid., 5:5). The novel emphasizes
the "partialities and injustice of her father's house" (29), and indeed it is one of the reasons Anne fell in love with Wentworth seven
years earlier: "She had hardly any body to love" (26). Her father
and sister prefer the company of Mrs Clay to Anne; as her sister puts
it, "She is nothing to me, compared with you" (145). When the
Elliots vacate Kellynch, to Anne falls the "trying" task of "going to almost every house in the parish, as a sort of take-leave" (39).

Anne's role in the family is summarized by the following ex-
change between Mary and Elizabeth, who decide that she should
go to Uppercross rather than to Bath: "'I cannot possibly do without Anne,' was Mary's reasoning; and Elizabeth's reply was, 'Then I
am sure Anne had better stay, for nobody will want her in Bath'"
(33). Amid the family squabbles at Uppercross, Anne fares little
better: "How was Anne to set all these matters to rights? She could
do little more than listen patiently, soften every grievance, and excuse each to the other; give them all hints of the forbearance necessary between such near neighbours" (46). Anne is left to take care
of the sick child, so that Mary and Charles can go to dinner at Uppercross Hall. That this suits Anne's plan for avoiding Wentworth
does not negate the fact that her sister makes use of her; and although Charles Musgrove can see that "it seems rather hard that
she should be left at home by herself, to nurse our sick child," he
ultimately finds it, however, "very agreeable" (58).

Similarly, Wentworth wants Anne to stay in Lyme to take care of
Louisa: "no one so proper, so capable as Anne" (114). In Bath, too,
Anne is made use of by her supposed friend, Mrs Smith, who "had
hoped to engage Anne's good offices with Mr Elliot" (210):

It immediately occurred, that something might be done in her favour by the
influence of the woman he loved, and she had been hastily preparing to interest Anne's feelings, as far as the observances due to Mr Elliot's character
would allow, when Anne's refutation of the supposed engagement changed
the face of every thing, and while it took from her the new-formed hope of
succeeding in the object of her first anxiety, left her at least the comfort of
telling the whole story her own way. (210–11)

Even Anne "could not but express some surprise at Mrs Smith's
having spoken of him so favourably" (211).

Ultimately, of course, everything turns around for the exploited
Anne Elliot, who undergoes a dramatic reversal of fortune. The
cameo, however, puts in the foreground what the main narrative
elides, namely, the exploitation that facilitates the happy resolu-

tion of the main narrative. The reunion of Wentworth and Anne is to a large degree based on Wentworth's accumulation of wealth and status. Comparable to that of Sir Thomas in *Mansfield Park*, Wentworth's newly found success and wealth are based on imperial activity. We never see this exploitation directly, but we do see the exploitation that Mrs Smith has suffered at the hands of Mr Elliot.

With the exception of the Gypsies in *Emma*, Mrs Smith is Austen's furthest look down the social ladder. Westgate Buildings, where Mrs Smith lives "in a very humble way, unable even to afford herself the comfort of a servant, and of course almost excluded from society" (152–3), is a place no one but Anne would ever visit. Although Mrs Russell approves of the visit, her offer of a carriage reflects a certain degree of hesitation: "Lady Russell, who entered thoroughly into her sentiments … was most happy to convey her *as near to Mrs Smith's lodgings in Westgate-buildings, as Anne chose to be taken*" (153; emphasis added). The offer implicitly suggests that Anne will, of course, have the tact not to let Mrs Russell's carriage take her all the way there: the carriage pulls up "near" Westgate (158). The distance between Anne's and Mrs Smith's worlds is emphasized by Sir Walter's incredulous response:

Westgate-buildings must have been rather surprised by the appearance of a carriage drawn up near its pavement! … Sir Henry Russell's widow, indeed, has no honours to distinguish her arms; but still, it is a handsome equipage, and no doubt is well known to convey a Miss Elliot. – A widow Mrs Smith, lodging in Westgate-buildings! – A poor widow, barely able to live, between thirty and forty – a mere Mrs Smith, an every day Mrs Smith. (157–8)

As Wiltshire points out, "Eighteenth-century Bath is a city of enclosure, Squares and Circuses of geometric design explicitly sequestering the gentry" (1992, 159) from "the lower classes who were necessary to its existence" (160). In this sense, *West*gate-buildings function in the same way as the *West* Indies, and the similarity in their names draws attention to this. The cameo narrative makes visible the exploitation that supplies Wentworth with his worth in the

main narrative. Hence the cameo dialogizes the main narrative; for
it reveals the oppression on which the success of the main narrative's hero is based.

The cameo invites us to compare *Persuasion*'s villainous Mr Elliot
to the heroic Captain Wentworth and to see them as similar rather
than opposites. As Mrs Smith tells us, Mr Elliot's first marriage was
motivated by his desire for "money, money" (Austen 1988, 5:202).
Similarly, his motivations for marrying Anne are inheritance and title. What Mr Elliot fails to gain, however, Wentworth achieves.
Wentworth's marriage to Anne completes his rise in the main narrative and society. The exploitative nature that we see in Mr Elliot,
both in terms of the cameo narrative and his courting of Anne, reveals the exploitative nature of Wentworth in the main narrative.
Mr Elliot dialogizes Wentworth. He reflects an image of the new
self-made man that the main narrative does not want to see and, indeed, cannot accommodate. Although the foolish Sir Walter is obsessed with mirrors, the rest of the characters seem to avoid their
reflections. One of the very few changes that Admiral Croft makes
at Kellynch is to remove some of these mirrors.

Ruth Perry argues that, "located in the aftermath of the extended struggle with France over colonial territory, *Persuasion* ro-
manticizes both the long contest and the objects of imperial
contention as a proving ground for British manhood" (1994, 101).
For Perry, *Persuasion*'s attitude towards colonialism is markedly different from that in *Mansfield Park*, and it "records a change of heart
about England's global destiny." She traces this "change of heart"
largely to biographical information; Austen "revised her estimation
of colonialism" because "she watched the wars of colonialism over
territory enable her brothers' upward mobility" (102): Wentworth,
"like Francis Austen, was defending England's colonial possessions
in the Caribbean, and the naval successes which enriched him, like
those that enriched Captain Austen, made it possible for him to
marry" (98). Hence Austen "found the colonialism's enabling of
class mobility very appealing." Perry claims that in *Persuasion*, "one
is never encouraged to feel that Wentworth's success is at the expense of the labor and property of colonized peoples although the

national project in which he proves his worth and makes his fortune is certainly a colonialist project" (103). The role of the cameo, however, is to "encourage" this awareness and to invite criticism of Wentworth's success.

Ironically, Mrs Smith's rise from Westgate is also facilitated by colonial possessions. Wentworth "recover[s] her husband's property in the West Indies" (Austen 1988, 5:251) so that at the end of the novel, Mrs Smith gains "improvement of income, with some improvement of health" (252) and, leaving Westgate firmly behind her, becomes Anne and Wentworth's "earliest visitor in their settled life" (251). Perry is confident that "Austen has no trouble imagining Mrs Smith enriched by property and slaves in another part of the world": Mrs Smith's story is cast as "another story of class triumph, where class has been imposed by gender. The property that Wentworth regains for the widow who lost all at her husband's death is, after all, her rightful inheritance and her inability to claim it has underscored her impotence as a woman. Mrs Smith has been victimized by a vicious aristocrat and been helped to her rightful West Indian property by a self-made man" (Perry 1994, 103). That the novel, however, does have "trouble" is made clear by the cameo narrative, which is an insistent reminder of life at the other side of town (Westgate) and the other end of the world (the West Indies). The main narrative's memory is selective, but the cameo does not permit such forgetfulness for the novel as a whole.

The recent film adaptation of *Persuasion* leaves the cameo out altogether. This rewriting is necessary to avoid any unflattering comparisons between Mr Elliot and Wentworth and to allow the image of the English ship on the high seas, the last shot in the film, to remain untainted. The film does not invite us to ask: "Where is that ship going?" Rather, the image speaks about freedom from the oppressive class structure embodied in Kellynch Hall, the triumph of the honest, rugged individual Wentworth, and the novel's empathy with the sentiments of the Romantic period. The advertisement of the film announces *Persuasion* as a great love story: "It's never too late for true love," reads the poster, and the fact that this interpretation cannot accommodate the cameo narrative reveals its potential danger.

These dramatic reversals of fortune are similar to the story of the "other" heroine. In the same manner that Louisa's fall facilitates Anne's rise in the narrative, Mr Elliot's wealth is based on Mrs Smith's poverty, while Wentworth's rise is facilitated by colonial exploitation, as is Mrs Smith's eventual turn for the better. By incorporating the challenges of the "other" heroine and the narrative cameo, Austen dialogizes the main narrative. Mr Elliot's "hollow and black" heart (which Mrs Smith reveals in the cameo) constitutes the violence that is buried in the text.

CHAPTER EIGHT

"We must forget it":
"The unhappy truth" in Pride and Prejudice

∼

Pride and Prejudice, Austen's "own darling Child" (Austen 1995, 201), is often considered the quintessential Austen novel, certainly the most widely read and most widely taught in schools and at the undergraduate level. As Marilyn Butler points out, "the general public has liked *Pride and Prejudice* the best of all Jane Austen's novels, and it is easy to see why" (1987, 217). Susan Morgan agrees that the novel "has a charmed place as the most popular of Austen's novels" (1980, 78). In criticism, too, the novel has held a privileged position: A. Walton Litz, for example, calls it "a summing up of her artistic career, a valedictory to the world of *Sense and Sensibility* and a token of things to come" (1965, 99).

In this discussion *Pride and Prejudice* has been far less central, giving way to the novel often considered its diametric opposite: *Mansfield Park.* Elizabeth triumphantly claims that Jane "only smiles, I laugh" (Austen 1988, 2:383), but Fanny Price does neither. For Lionel Trilling, "no small part" of *Mansfield Park*'s "interest derives from the fact that it seems to controvert everything" that *Pride and Prejudice* "tells us about life": the latter "celebrates … spiritedness, vivacity, celerity, and lightness," while "almost the opposite can be said" of *Mansfield Park* (1955, 211). Time has proven Austen right: "I am very strongly haunted by the idea that to those Readers who have preferred P&P. it will appear inferior in Wit, & to those who have preferred MP. very inferior in good Sense" (Austen 1995, 306). Austen's famous remark to her sister Cassandra that *Pride and Prejudice* is "rather too light & bright & sparkling; – it wants shade" has often been read without its irony:

It wants to be stretched out here & there with a long Chapter – of sense if it could be had, if not of solemn specious nonsense – about something unconnected with the story; an Essay on Writing, a critique on Walter Scott, or the history of Buonaparte – or anything that would form a contrast & bring the reader with increased delight to the playfulness & Epigrammatism of the general stile. – I doubt your quite agreeing with me here – I know your starched Notions. (Ibid., 203)

That *Pride and Prejudice* is considered Austen's best or most perfect novel has a lot more to do with preconceived assumptions about Austen than with the novel itself. As Claudia Johnson points out, "We will certainly misrepresent her accomplishment if we posit this singular novel as the typical one against which the others are to be judged" (1988, 93).

In the case of Elizabeth and Darcy, love conquers all. Their union, critics argue, is achieved by displacing class and economic realities onto secondary characters and plots. For Mary Poovey, "the realistic elements" are "carefully contained" (1984, 202). The love between Darcy and Elizabeth "not only overcomes all obstacles; it brings about a perfect society" by the end of the story (201): "With Darcy at its head and Elizabeth at its heart, society will apparently be able to contain the anarchic impulses of individualism and humanize the rigidities of prejudice, and everyone – even Miss Bingley – will live more or less happily in the environs of Pemberley, the vast estate whose permanence, prominence, and unique and uniquely satisfying fusion of individual taste and utility, of nature and art, symbolize Jane Austen's ideal" (202). According to Judith Lowder Newton, "For all its reference to money and money matters, for all its consciousness of economic fact and economic influence, *Pride and Prejudice* is devoted not to establishing but to denying the force of economics in human life. In the reading of the novel the real *force* of economics simply melts away" (1981, 61). Common to these interpretations is the idea that Austen displaces her social realism and social criticism in order to present a utopian ending "with an air of credibility which lends force to the spell of the fantasy upon us" (85).[1]

Indeed, *Pride and Prejudice* presents a particular challenge. Of all the novels, it comes closest to reconciling the individual with society, the very project with which Austen is usually associated. Even a critic like Johnson, whose readings seek to redeem Austen from charges of conservatism, is somewhat baffled by *Pride and Prejudice*. Agreeing with Poovey that the "markedly fairy-tale-like quality" (1988, 74) of the novel is "almost shamelessly wish fulfilling" (73), she struggles to argue that the novel is not, therefore, "politically suspect" (74): "Austen consents to conservative myths, but only in order to possess them and to ameliorate them from within, so that the institutions they vindicate can bring about, rather than inhibit, the expansion and the fulfilment of happiness" (93). Yet in her conclusion Johnson admits that the novel is "a conservative enterprise, after all" (92): it is "profoundly conciliatory ... and of all Austen's novels it most affirms established social arrangements without damaging their prestige or fundamentally challenging their wisdom or equity" (73–4). We can, however, uncover some disturbances to a novel often considered "categorically happy" (73) by bringing the cameo narrative to the fore.

The challenges of the past are displaced or resolved only if we read *Pride and Prejudice* monologically and ignore the dialogism facilitated by the cameo. The main narrative requires characters and readers to forgive and forget, but the cameo vengefully offers a reminder of the past. In his introduction to Bakhtin's *Problems of Dostoevsky's Poetics*, Wayne Booth admits that he has "often scoffed about modes of criticism that care so little about formal construction that they would be unaffected if the works discussed had been

---

1 Two notable exceptions to the readings of *Pride and Prejudice* as a "happy" novel of reconciliation are Susan Fraiman's "The Humiliation of Elizabeth Bennet" and Paula Bennett's "Family Plots." Fraiman discusses the homosocial trading of Elizabeth between Mr Bennet and Darcy. Bennett draws on family systems theory to explore the dysfunctional nature of Elizabeth's family.

written backward"; yet much of Bakhtin's criticism "would not be affected if we discovered new manuscripts that scrambled the order of events, or the handling of flashbacks and foreshadowings, or the manipulations of point of view. It is not linear sequence but the touch of the author at each moment that matters. What we seek is what might be called the best *vertical* structure, rather than a given temporal structure and its technical transformations" (1984, xxv). If we refuse to follow the main narrative's linearity and temporal progression towards reconciliation and instead place the "handling of flashbacks" in the foreground, then we arrive at a very different text, a dialogic text, in which the narrative cameo holds equal weight with the main narrative. Such an interpretation, which could be construed as reading *Pride and Prejudice* as if it "had been written backward," registers the novel's dialogism. The main narrative is based on a reconciliation of the past and the present, but if the reader refuses to become co-opted into this monologic narrative, then *Pride and Prejudice*'s happy ending emerges as fragile and conditional indeed.

In his letter of vindication to Elizabeth, Darcy tries to explain his interference in Jane and Bingley's relationship, and he gives a history of Wickham: "My character required it to be written and read" (Austen 1988, 2:196). Darcy's narrative is, of course, in direct contrast to the one circulated by Wickham earlier in the novel. Darcy reveals the profligate behaviour of Mr Wickham, culminating in his attempt to seduce Georgiana, then only fifteen years old: "Mr Wickham's chief object was unquestionably my sister's fortune, which is thirty thousand pounds; but I cannot help supposing that the hope of revenging himself on me, was a strong inducement." Georgiana confided in her brother, who fortunately averted the crisis: Mr Wickham "left the place immediately" (202).

This past, rather than being contained in the cameo, repeats itself. Wickham reincurs massive debts and seduces and elopes with Lydia. Again Mr Darcy rescues the situation and bribes Wickham to marry Lydia. The cameo narrative points out the vulnerability of the heroine. Like Marianne Dashwood and Anne Elliot, who closely escape the villains of their respective novels, Elizabeth narrowly avoids the dangerous consequences of her flirtation with Wickham.

Moreover, the cameo brings out the anxieties surrounding the marriage of Elizabeth and Darcy. The plot of Wickham, the fortune-hunter in pursuit of Georgiana and Pemberley, presents an unflattering parallel to Elizabeth's aspirations towards Pemberley: "She felt, that to be mistress of Pemberley might be something!" (245). As Susan Fraiman points out, there is an "element ... of crass practicality": "Elizabeth is appalled by Charlotte's pragmatism, and yet, choosing Darcy over Wickham, she is herself beguiled by the entrepreneurial marriage plot" (1989, 182). Lady Catherine de Bourgh would agree. The narrative cameo aligns Elizabeth and Wickham and almost sets them in competition with one another. Wickham's failed attempt to win Georgiana's fortune and his consolation prize (Lydia) shed an interrogative light on Elizabeth's success. The main narrative insists that Elizabeth's motives are noble, but the cameo contaminates this purity, since ultimately Elizabeth gets the very thing to which Wickham has aspired. Darcy states that Wickham was motivated by greed and "the hope of revenging himself on me" (Austen 1988, 2:202). In a sense, Elizabeth achieves the ultimate revenge. Once considering Elizabeth "not handsome enough to tempt *me*" (12), Darcy finds himself "tortured" (367) into humility and love. The relationship and confidence between Wickham and Elizabeth in the first half of the novel should not be dismissed or underestimated. In the end Wickham, too, profits by Elizabeth's infiltration of Pemberley. The cameo raises Lady Catherine's question (357): "Are the shades of Pemberley to be thus polluted?"

Mr Darcy is remarkably possessive of the information the narrative cameo contains. Indeed, he has a lot at stake – the sanctity and mystique of Pemberley and its inhabitants: "To no creature had it been revealed, where secrecy was possible, except to Elizabeth." Darcy is "particularly anxious to conceal it" from Bingley due to his "wish which Elizabeth had long ago attributed to him" (270) of joining Georgiana's and Bingley's fortunes. Darcy needs to erase any memories of Georgiana's misconduct and any memories that suggest the gullibility of the Pemberley residents (Darcy's father, sister, and, finally, himself). In the light of Darcy's succumbing to Elizabeth – "In vain have I struggled" (189) – this is particularly important. Thus Wickham's behaviour in the cameo has to be forgotten, because it brings up the very questions that the main narrative has to elide in order to achieve its "fairy-tale-like quality." This applies equally to Darcy and to Elizabeth; he needs to maintain his image as a responsible and discriminating estate owner, and Elizabeth needs to present herself as marrying "only" for love. The cameo narrative's presence, however, continually disrupts these constructions and the main narrative's closure. Fraiman interprets Darcy as an author whose letter "monopoliz[es] the narrative" (1989, 176) and "in a play for literary hegemony (to be author and critic both), tells us how to read him" (176–7), leaving Elizabeth vanquished and humiliated: "Against the broad chest of Darcy's logic, Elizabeth beats the ineffectual fists of her own" (177). Elizabeth, however, has an equal stake in regulating the letter.

There are constant reminders of the past throughout the novel. Georgiana's presence is a case in point. At a gathering at Pemberley, Miss Bingley "took the first opportunity of saying with sneering civility" to Elizabeth, "Pray, Miss Eliza, are not the – shire militia removed from Meryton? They must be a great loss to *your* family." Elizabeth sees the unintended effect on Darcy and Georgiana: "An involuntary glance showed Darcy with an heightened complexion, earnestly looking at her, and his sister overcome with confusion, and unable to lift up her eyes." "Had Miss Bingley known what pain she was then giving her beloved friend, she undoubtedly would have refrained from the hint" (Austen 1988, 2:269), but "not a syllable had ever reached her of Miss Darcy's meditated elopement" (269–70). This episode registers the inherently disruptive power of the past, which cannot be contained in "secrecy."

Like Mr Elliot in *Persuasion*, Wickham is a family member who is permanently married to the main narrative. Despite Mr Bennet's initial opposition, the prodigal son-in-law is received at Longbourn.

Lydia visits Pemberley, and both Lydia and Wickham stay at Nether-
field, "frequently ... so long, that even Bingley's good humour was
overcome, and he proceeded so far as to *talk* of giving them a hint
to be gone." Darcy "for Elizabeth's sake ... assisted ... [Wickham]
farther in his profession," and both Elizabeth and Jane are regu-
larly "applied to, for some little assistance towards discharging their
bills" (387). Although they are "banished to the North" (314), they
are an integral part of the family circle. This is very different from
Mansfield Park, in which no attempt is made to "rescue" Maria
Bertram, whose banishment is permanent: Sir Thomas does not
grant her visitation rights.

   To accomplish *Pride and Prejudice*'s family reunion, Wickham's
past has to be erased. Jane is "thankful ... that we never let them
know what has been said against him; we must forget it ourselves"
(274). Although Elizabeth argues that "'Their conduct has been
such ... as neither you, nor I, nor any body, can ever forget'" (305),
she firmly avoids the topic: "Come, Mr Wickham, we are brother
and sister, you know. Do not let us quarrel about the past" (329).
Johnson argues that the novel's "conclusion preserves the heroines' friendships and promises the mutual regard of husbands and
relations": "The band of good friends is all related by marriage in
the end, but they are not good friends because they are related – as
conservative apologists would have it – rather they are good relations because they were good friends first" (1988, 92). Johnson
clearly overlooks the presence of Wickham, but Austen goes out of
her way to include him.

   At the end of the novel, Elizabeth and Darcy discuss Darcy's letter. Elizabeth reassures him that all is forgiven: "The letter, perhaps, began in bitterness, but it did not end so. The adieu is charity
itself. But think no more of the letter. The feelings of the person
who wrote, and the person who received it, are now so widely different from what they were then, that every unpleasant circumstance
attending it, ought to be forgotten. You must learn some of my philosophy. Think only of the past as its remembrance gives you pleasure" (368–9). *Pride and Prejudice* itself functions like this letter; the
novel's memory is highly selective. Wickham, however morally

bankrupt, is no longer a threat and is recuperated into a highly comic ending, becoming Mr Bennet's "favourite" (379) son-in-law. Similarly, when Jane, expressing concern for Elizabeth's acceptance of Darcy, says, "I know how much you dislike him" (372), Elizabeth replies: "*That* is all to be forgot. Perhaps I did not always love him so well as I do now. But in such cases as these, a good memory is unpardonable. This is the last time I shall ever remember it myself" (373). The novel follows the structure of comedic reversal: "The Bennets were speedily pronounced to be the luckiest family in the world, though only a few weeks before, when Lydia had first run away, they had been generally proved to be marked out for misfortune" (350). Like *Persuasion*, *Pride and Prejudice* is a novel about second chances, but neither Elizabeth nor Jane nor Lydia suffer in the way Anne Elliot does.

Austen points out the selective memory that is required to believe that at the end of the novel we have a "perfect society" (Poovey 1984, 201). "Though Darcy could never receive *him* at Pemberley" (Austen 1988, 2:387), Wickham and the remembrance of the past cast a shadow over Pemberley. Like the narrative cameos in *Sense and Sensibility* and *Persuasion*, the tale of Wickham and Georgiana is a vehicle for dialogism, for it reminds us of material that the main narrative represses. *Mansfield Park* and *Northanger Abbey* are similarly haunted by tales of violence.

PART THREE

"Grievous imprisonment of body and mind":
Investigating Crimes

∾

Even the smooth surface of the family-union seems worth preserving, though there may be nothing durable beneath. (*Persuasion*, Austen 1988, 5:198)

However taboo the subject of family violence was and still is, Austen was by no means unfamiliar with it. Claire Tomalin's and David Nokes's biographies are valuable corrections to the overstated tranquility of Austen's life. It has been suggested by a range of biographers such as Nokes, John Halperin, and Jane Aiken Hodge that Lady Craven, the grandmother of Jane Austen's friends Martha and Mary Lloyd, formed the model for Lady Susan in the fragment of that name: "For her character, Jane Austen had almost certainly gone back to the stories the Lloyd girls could tell about their mother and aunts' sufferings at the hands of the unnatural Lady Craven" (Hodge 1972, 44). Lady Craven, "all tenderness to her children in public, in private beat and starved and locked them up" (Kronenberger 1969, 193), and "three of her daughters had fled from home to escape her despotic rule" (Nokes 1997, 152). Referred to as "the cruel Mrs Craven" (Jenkins 1938, 116), she was a well-known scandalous figure in Austen's time. Whether she is the model for Austen's fictional character is open to question (Park Honan [1987] and Claire Tomalin [1997] suggest the influence of Austen's cousin Eliza de Feuillide), but Lady Craven does serve as a reminder that issues of abuse and assault are not the product of a twentieth-century sensibility. As Anna Clark reveals in *Women's Silence, Men's Violence: Sexual Assault in England, 1770–1845* (1987), violence towards adult women and children was a highly debated topic then as it is now.

This section highlights tales of violence that dialogize the main narratives of *Mansfield Park* and *Northanger Abbey*, the ones that criticism has chosen to valorize. *Mansfield Park*'s Fanny Price is examined as a survivor of domestic violence. Such a reading directly contradicts the narrative that constructs her and, by extension, the novel as the embodiment of conservative values. The discussion of *Northanger Abbey* examines the text's ambiguity regarding Catherine's suspicions about the general and focuses on the narrative that dialogizes the one that punishes and schools Catherine's imagination. The section concludes by demonstrating that the "Wicked Mother" (Horwitz 1989, 181) in *Lady Susan* is not anomalous. The parental coercion and violence that the fragment exposes is also implicit in the depictions of family life in *Mansfield Park* and *Northanger Abbey*.

CHAPTER NINE

"No tread of violence was ever heard": Silent Suffering in Mansfield Park

∼

Louis Althusser argues that although what he called ideological state apparatuses "function massively and predominantly *by ideology* … they also function secondarily by repression, even if ultimately, but only ultimately, this is very attenuated and concealed, even symbolic" (1971, 138). While ideological state apparatuses primarily disseminate ideology into the "*private* domain," they also exercise the violence characteristic of the "Repressive State Apparatus," which "belongs entirely to the *public* domain" (137) and which "functions massively and predominantly *by repression*": "Schools and Churches use suitable methods of punishment, expulsion, selection, etc., to 'discipline' not only their shepherds, but also their flocks. The same is true of the Family" (138).

The distinction between "public" and "private," says Althusser, is "internal to bourgeois law, and valid in the (subordinate) domains in which bourgeois law exercises its 'authority'" (137). Yet the state is "neither public nor private; on the contrary, it is the precondition for any distinction between the public and private." So it is with state ideological apparatuses: "It is unimportant whether the institutions in which they are realized are 'public' or 'private.' What matters is how they function" (138). Thus, the events within the privacy of Mansfield Park are inextricably linked to the events in the public realm. While *Mansfield Park* is ostensibly a novel of education or of growing up within a family, it is also a novel about repression. The "symbolic" acts of violence towards Fanny Price maintain the ideology of Mansfield Park, which is perpetrated both publicly and privately by both ideological and repressive apparatuses.

In *Sense and Sensibility*, Jane Austen writes, "On every formal visit a child ought to be of the party, by way of provision for discourse" (1988, 1:31). Apart from "provision for discourse," children do not figure prominently in the novels.[1] As the young Austen puts it in "Edgar and Emma," "Their Children were too numerous to be particularly described; it is sufficient to say that in general they were virtuously inclined & not given to any wicked ways" (6:31). Austen heroines typically enter at the marriagable age; the first paragraph of *Northanger Abbey*, describing Catherine's fondness for "rolling down the green slope at the back of the house" (5:14), is a brief exception. *Mansfield Park*'s Fanny Price enters the novel as a child, "just ten years old" (3:12), and a significant section of the novel focuses on Fanny's childhood experience, suggesting that it is one of *Mansfield Park*'s important themes. Fanny is transplanted from the poor parental home to that of the rich relatives, Sir Thomas and Lady Bertram; in Edward Said's terms, she is "imported" (1993, 91).

Said's influential discussion of the novel's references to Antigua reflects the current interest in situating Austen in the context of empire.[2] Said discusses how "Thomas Bertram's slave plantation in Antigua is mysteriously necessary to the poise and the beauty of Mansfield Park."[3] By "sublimat[ing] the agonies of Caribbean existence to a mere half dozen passing references to Antigua" (59),

---

1 Juliet McMaster argues that in *Emma* children "have their important though unobtrusive role to play in the action" (1992, 62). Austen's characterization of children in the novel reveals her engagement with not only the "cultural movement towards a recognition of the status of childhood" but also the "cult of the child as developed by Wordsworth and the other Romantic poets": Austen "shows children not as merely tentative, liminal souls, nor as retarded adults, but as beings who are developing firm little identities of their own. She records and remembers their sex, names and habits. She recognizes childhood as a separate state with its own tastes and appealing characteristics" (63).

2 *Mansfield Park*'s participation in colonial discourse has been commented on by Patrick Brantlinger, Meenakshi Mukherjee, Brian Southam, Moira Ferguson, Maaja A. Stewart, Joseph Lew, and, perhaps most influentially, Edward Said in *Culture and Imperialism*.

3 Ruth Perry claims that "Edward Said has condemned Austen's attitudes towards slavery and colonialism as unconscious and unquestioning" and that he "accuses Austen of referring to Antigua and to the slave trade casually, merely by way of adding decor to her story of domestic rearrangements" (1994, 100). Said's project, however, is not to "accuse" Austen or "condemn" her novel, which he calls "brilliant" (1993, 96): "This by no

Austen takes part in creating a "structure of attitude and reference" that posits England as the centre and the colonies as extensions to be exploited. Said goes on to say that "the right to colonial possessions helps directly to establish social order and moral priorities at home" (62); that is, the novel "aligned the holding of power and privilege abroad with comparable activities at home" (76). Similarly, Moira Ferguson argues that "power relations within the community of Mansfield Park re-enact and refashion plantocratic paradigms" (1993, 70). In *Mansfield Park* the colonization of Antigua is linked to the colonization of Fanny Price's mind and body: both are crucial to the maintenance of Mansfield Park. Even though the analysis of the intersection of imperialism and patriarchy has produced great insight, Fanny's history of neglect and abuse at the hands of family has been consistently minimized. Here I investigate the instances of domestic violence and present a rereading of the novel's troubling closure in the light of that violence.

While Mrs Norris's cruelty is more visible than anyone else's in the novel, it is important to remember that her behaviour is sanctioned by Sir Thomas, who asked her to "assist us in our endeavours to choose exactly the right line of conduct": Mrs Norris "was quite at his service" (Austen 1988, 3:11). The anxiety about the "right line of conduct" towards Fanny is an anxiety about class; Sir Thomas and Mrs Norris agree that "there will be some difficulty in our way ... as to the distinction proper to be made" (10). Throughout the novel, it is clear that Fanny is a potential threat. She must be made to feel inferior so as not to aspire to one of Sir Thomas's sons or the position that is reserved for her cousins Maria and Julia;

---

means involves hurling critical epithets at European or, generally, Western art and culture by way of wholesale condemnation ... What I want to examine is how the processes of imperialism occurred beyond the level of economic laws and political decisions, and ... were manifested at another very significant level, that of the national culture" (12–13). Said insists that "understanding that connection does not reduce or diminish the novels' value as works of art: on the contrary, because of their *worldliness*, because of their complex affiliations with their real setting, they are *more* interesting and *more* valuable as works of art" (13).

she must be kept down, for her own good, of course, Sir Thomas would argue. Thus, it is crucial that he rewrite Fanny's childhood:

I am aware that there has been sometimes, in some points, a misplaced distinction; but I think too well of you, Fanny, to suppose you will ever harbour resentment on that account. – You have an understanding, which will prevent you from receiving things only in part, and judging partially by the event. – You will take in the whole of the past, you will consider times, persons, and probabilities, and you will feel that *they* were not the least your friends who were educating and preparing you for that mediocrity of condition which *seemed* to be your lot ... it was kindly meant ... But enough of this. (313)

While Sir Thomas is ostensibly speaking about Mrs Norris, the shift to "*they*" makes it clear that he is including himself. Sir Thomas legitimizes Mrs Norris and himself by repeatedly stressing that it was for Fanny's "own good," thereby erasing Fanny's history of neglect. I agree with Johnson's assessment that *Mansfield Park* "appears to let conservative ideologues have it their way ... only to give them the chance ... to discredit themselves with their own voices" (1988, 120). My reading explores the narrative of child abuse as one of the ways in which the text discredits conservative ideologues. Rather than taking in the whole of Fanny's past, as Sir Thomas would like us to do, let us look at specific "events."

Although Mrs Norris claims that "I should hate myself if I were capable of neglecting her" (7), she takes great pleasure in the humiliation of Fanny, reminding her continually of her dependence and "uncommon good fortune in having such friends" (10). When the Bertram girls think Fanny "prodigiously stupid," for she "cannot put the map of Europe together or ... tell the principal rivers in Russia" (18), Mrs Norris is eager to flatter them at the expense of Fanny: "You are blessed with wonderful memories, and your poor cousin has probably none at all" (19). Examples of Mrs Norris's emotional abuse of Fanny abound in the text.[4] Mrs Norris exploits

---

4 See Juliet McMaster's discussion of Mrs Norris's verbal abuse in "The Talkers and Listeners of *Mansfield Park*" (1995).

Fanny for her own purposes: by exalting Julia and Maria at Fanny's expense, Mrs Norris hopes to ingratiate herself with Sir Thomas and Lady Bertram, on whose wealth she is constantly preying.

No one at Mansfield seems to object to this behaviour. In fact, Mrs Norris sets an example of what is deemed acceptable conduct towards Fanny; she "assisted to form [Julia and Maria's] minds" (19) about Fanny. Even Edmund, whom Fanny thinks of as her advocate, seems to be oblivious to Mrs Norris's cruelty. Terrified at the prospect of moving in with her Aunt Norris, Fanny receives little sympathy from Edmund, who considers it an excellent plan: "I hope it does not distress you very much" (26). The only characters who think Fanny ill treated are the Crawfords.[5] Significantly, those who recognize Fanny's habitualized oppression are outside of the Mansfield family.

Mrs Norris's cruelty goes beyond her continual emotional abuse of Fanny; repeatedly, we see her punishment of Fanny's body. While all the other family members receive the benefits of heat, Mrs Norris ensures that Fanny's "East room" (151), her "nest of comforts" (152), remains cold, thereby curtailing not only Fanny's bodily comfort but also her access to private space: "It was habitable in many an early spring, and late autumn morning, to such a willing mind as Fanny's, and while there was a gleam of sunshine, she hoped not to be driven from it entirely, even when winter came" (151). Fanny's space is continually infringed upon. Mrs Norris makes her walk beyond her physical endurance, and when as a result she lies ill with headache and exhaustion, she is scolded: "That is a very foolish trick, Fanny, to be idling away all the evening upon a sofa ... You should learn to think of other people" (71).

John Wiltshire makes a very interesting connection: "The use both aunts make of Fanny, 'standing and stooping in a hot sun' might call to mind the use Sir Thomas, now in Antigua, makes of

5 See my discussion of Mary Crawford in Part One. Even Henry Crawford, with all his faults, realizes that the Bertrams should "be heartily ashamed of their own abominable neglect and unkindness" (Austen 1988, 3:297).

his slaves" (1992, 72). Moira Ferguson notes that Mrs Norris's "surname recalls John Norris, one of the most vile proslaveryites of the day." Austen "was well aware of Norris's notoriety, having read Thomas Clarkson's celebrated *History of the Abolition of the Slave Trade* in which Norris is categorically condemned ... while she was working out the plot of *Mansfield Park*" (1993, 70). Furthermore, as Margaret Kirkham (1987) and Ferguson point out, the novel's title clearly alludes to the Mansfield Judgment of 1772: "The decision stipulated that no slaves could be forcibly returned from Britain to the Caribbean, which was widely interpreted to mean that slavery in Britain had been legally abolished. Austen's invocation of Lord Mansfield's name ... suggests the novel's intrinsic engagement with slavery" (Ferguson 1993, 82). As Brian Southam points out in "The Silence of the Bertrams" (1995), during the composition of the novel and the time span that the novel covers, "the 'slave trade' was still a burning issue, a persistent and horrifying scandal, debated in Parliament and extensively reported and discussed in the newspapers and periodicals" (13).[6] Mrs Norris's name and the novel's title reflect Austen's engagement with issues of slavery.

---

6 Southam (1995) points out that "the Austens too had a dependence, however slight, upon the prosperity of a plantation in Antigua; and events similar to the *Mansfield Park* story would have become known to Jane Austen in her childhood":

> In 1760, Jane's father, the Revd George Austen, was appointed principal trustee of a plantation in Antigua, a fact unmentioned in the family biographies and memoirs. During Jane Austen's lifetime, the full abomination of slavery struck the nation's conscience and the "harshness and despotism" of the plantation owners and their managers were reported back to the family by Francis Austen from his experience of naval duty in the West Indies. A silence not unlike the "dead silence" at Mansfield Park may have begun to gather over Mr Austen's West Indian connections – connections which extended deeper into the household. The owner of the Antigua plantation, James Langford Nibbs, a former pupil of Mr Austen at Oxford, stood in 1765 as godfather for James, the eldest Austen son. Like Sir Thomas Bertram, Mr Nibbs had a spendthrift elder son, James junior; and like Tom Bertram, James junior was taken off to Antigua by his father to detach him from his "unwholesome connections." (14)

For further connections between the Austen family and colonialism, see Frank Gibbon's "The Antiguan Connection" (1982) and Ruth Perry's "Austen and Empire: A Thinking Woman's Guide to British Imperialism" (1994).

Even once Fanny begins to move from the margins of the household to the centre, ultimately becoming the upholder of Mansfield
Park, she never unlearns the lesson of her insignificance.
Mrs Norris has trained her well, for she is constantly in the agoniz-
ing state of "painful gratitude" (Austen 1988, 3:322): "Like a grateful slave she lets particular and small acts of kindness overshadow a
larger act of cruelty" (Johnson 1988, 108). When she finally receives heat in her attic, "she was struck, quite struck ... it seemed
too much" (Austen 1988, 3:322). For Fanny, happiness is never un-
alloyed. Every gift reinforces her feeling of indebtedness. When
Edmund, recognizing the "ill effects" (36) of lack of exercise, lends
Fanny one of his three horses, she "regarded her cousin as an example of every thing good and great ... and as entitled to such gratitude from her, as no feelings could be strong enough to pay" (37).
The horse, of course, also brings her pain, for once Miss Crawford
asks to ride it, Fanny's claim to it becomes secondary: "She won-
dered that Edmund should forget her, and felt a pang" (67).
William's gift of the cross is emblematic of Fanny's position within
the family structure (both at Mansfield and Portsmouth): family is
the cross she bears. To go with the cross, she needs a chain. She is
offered two chains as gifts, again highly appropriate, for the gifts reflect her imprisonment, deprivation, and indebtedness. For Fanny
Price, gifts have strings attached; the cross has a chain. Miss
Crawford gives her the gift of a chain, but it is used to allow Henry
to make unwanted advances towards Fanny. Once Fanny realizes
this, the gift becomes a burden – a cross she, however, has to bear.
She cannot return it – that would be ungrateful – and it becomes
truly unbearable when Edmund looks at the gift as further evidence of the superior claims of Mary Crawford and insists that
Fanny wear it.

The meaning of the cross and chains becomes fully apparent in
the scenes that witness Fanny's body displayed and examined and
Fanny humiliated, silenced, and powerless. Sir Thomas's preoccupation with Fanny's body and her obvious discomfort are significant
in the context of Fanny's symptoms of abuse and the novel's engagement with the discourse of colonialism. They are indeed, as

Johnson refers to them, "disturbing" (1988, 118): "Austen's depiction of family life was immensely daring ... insofar as it is shown to
be a place not free from but sometimes uncomfortably saturated in
erotic feeling" (1995, 67). These scenes have not received adequate
critical attention, yet they are crucial to our understanding of the
novel, particularly Fanny's loyalty and "inheritance" of Mansfield
Park. They are scenes of sexual abuse both in their immediate context and in the memories to which they allude.[7] Fanny is most afraid
of Sir Thomas. Upon her uncle's return from Antigua, "her agitation and alarm exceeded all that was endured by the rest ... She was
nearly fainting: all her former habitual dread of her uncle was returning" (Austen 1988, 3:176). She pulls herself together "to per-
form the dreadful duty" of appearing before him (177):

Sir Thomas was at that moment looking round him, and saying "But where
is Fanny? – Why do not I see my little Fanny?", and on perceiving her, came
forward with a kindness which astonished and penetrated her, calling her
his dear Fanny, kissing her affectionately, and observing with decided pleasure how much she was grown! ... He led her nearer the light and looked at

---

7 This may seem an odd argument to make, for Austen's novels have repeatedly been
noted and patronized for their lack of sex. In "'A Pair of Fine Eyes': Jane Austen's Treatment of Sex" (1975), Alice Chandler provides a potent antidote to this critical common-
place: "*Mansfield Park*, Marvin Mudrick's shrine of the sexual taboo and Kingsley Amis's
palace of prudery, is curiously rich in sex symbols – perhaps because it is more of a hot-
house than a refrigerator" (93). Her reading is based on "studying Jane Austen's 'indirection,'" which made her aware "of the limited range of explicit statement allowed to a
novelist of her generation ... For a woman, of course, the problem was compounded"
(89). Arguing that "sexual implications abound in *Mansfield Park*" (93), Chandler discusses literary allusions to *Lovers' Vows* and Shakespeare's *Henry VIII* (90), which are not shy
about sex. She suggests that Austen deliberately chose a heroine's name with sexual implications: "Fanny Price ... comes from Crabbe's *Parish Register*, where Fanny Price is a
chaste and lovely maiden, who resists a sexually eager young squire to marry the pure
youth of her choice" (90); the name is also "eighteenth-century and ... modern British
slang [for] female pudendum" (92). Moreover, Fanny Price shares her first name with
Fanny Hill, the carefully named heroine of John Cleland's notorious *Memoirs of a Woman
of Pleasure* (1748-49), a text abundant and explicit in sexual matters. In *Jane Austen on Love*
(1978), Juliet McMaster also argues that the novels are sexually charged: "I find it hard
to credit that anyone who has read *Pride and Prejudice* could subscribe to the view of Miss
Austen as an old maid who wrote sexless novels" (48-9).

her again – inquired particularly after her health, and then correcting himself, observed, that he need *not* inquire, for her appearance spoke sufficiently on that point. (177–8)

Pulling her "nearer the light," he surveys Fanny's body, to her obvious discomfort and confusion; she "knew not how to feel, nor where to look. She was quite oppressed" (178). Sir Thomas's preoccupation with Fanny's body is evident again in Edmund's testimony:

Ask your uncle what he thinks, and you will hear compliments enough; and though they may be chiefly on your person, you must put up with it, and trust to his seeing as much beauty of mind in time ... Your uncle thinks you very pretty, dear Fanny ... Your complexion is so improved! – and you have gained so much countenance! – and your figure – Nay, Fanny, do not turn away about it – it is but an uncle. If you cannot bear an uncle's admiration what is to become of you? You must really begin to harden yourself to the idea of being worth looking at. (197–8)

Lastly, here is Fanny taking refuge from her suitor, Henry Crawford, in her little attic:

Nearly half an hour had passed, and she was growing very comfortable, when suddenly the sound of a step in regular approach was heard – a heavy step, an unusual step in that part of the house; it was her uncle's; she knew it as well as his voice; she had trembled at it as often, and began to tremble again, at the idea of his coming up to speak to her, whatever might be the subject. – It was indeed Sir Thomas, who opened the door, and asked if she were there, and if he might come in. The terror of his former occasional visits to that room seemed all renewed, and she felt as if he were going to examine her again in French and English. (312)

These scenes are important because they reveal the power dynamic characteristic of sexual abuse: all Fanny can do is tremble with fear; she cannot question her uncle's power; she cannot retreat to a safe space.

These scenes need to be highlighted because in and of themselves they constitute abuse. As Sandra Butler explains, the "diverse forms" of incestuous assault "include any sexual activity or experience imposed on a child which results in emotional, physical or sexual trauma": acts of incestuous assault "are not always genital and the experience not always a physical one" (Butler 1985, 5).[8] Fanny's subjection to sexual remarks and scrutiny and her visible discomfort and anxiety fall very much within the parameters of this definition. The minimizing of Austen's portrayal of violence reflects our culture's high threshold of toleration for domestic violence, where none but the most extreme cases are considered "violent." These instances, furthermore, are worth investigating because they suggest scenes not directly represented in the text: "the terror of his former occasional visits." This "reality" is also indirectly expressed by Fanny's trauma symptoms, which the novel clearly documents.

Fanny is distinguished from the other Austen heroines by physical weakness. Emma is "the complete picture of grown-up health" (Austen 1988, 4:39), Elizabeth Bennet's purposeful walk across a field gives "brilliancy ... to her complexion" (2:33), and Catherine Morland at the opening of *Northanger Abbey* "loved nothing so well in the world as rolling down the green slope at the back of the house" (5:14). Marianne Dashwood in *Sense and Sensibility* does get very ill but recovers her robust health once she submits to moral education, and the pale Anne Elliot of *Persuasion* is reborn with "the bloom and freshness of youth restored" (5:104). The Austen heroines are all great walkers, in contrast to the hypochondriacs, like the Parker sisters in "Sanditon," Mrs Bennet of *Pride and Prejudice*, and such parodied ideals of feminine passivity as Fanny's aunt, Lady Bertram, who seems physically attached to the sofa. Fanny Price again is the exception: she "is the only one of Jane Austen's heroines whose body is frail, 'debilitated' or 'enfeebled'" (Wiltshire 1992, 63). Fanny's symptoms of trauma are often naturalized as her inherent "weak character," and this perceived passiv-

8 See also Judith Lewis Herman's *Father-Daughter Incest* (1981).

ity, frailty, and reticence continue to make her the least popular Austen heroine. Trilling announced with confidence: "Nobody, I believe, has ever found it possible to like the heroine of *Mansfield Park*" (1955, 212). His opinion has been seconded by many others; as Marilyn Butler puts it, "That Fanny is a failure is widely agreed" (1987, 248). For Nina Auerbach, Fanny is a "particularly unaccommodating heroine" (1985, 23), "a killjoy, a blighter of ceremonies and divider of families" (25). By extension, *Mansfield Park*, with its so-called "Difficulty Beauty" (Edwards 1987, 7), is the least popular of Austen's novels. The common critical insensitivity to Fanny's suffering denies the violent nature of the novel. Over and over, we see Fanny faint, weak, pale, and "in excessive trembling" (Austen 1988, 3:176). These physical responses are manifestations of exhaustion, agitation, and fear; they are "sign[s] of her subordinate social and moral status" (Wiltshire 1992, 64). Victimized twice, Fanny is made to be afraid and then punished for seeming weak and timid.

Critics often suggest that Fanny has a degree of choice – that she willingly participates in her oppression. According to Margaret Kirkham, Austen "teases us about Miss Fanny" (1987, 117) and "laughs at Fanny when she herself acquiesces, as she often does, in the submissive role in which an unjust domestic 'order' has cast her" (126). Moira Ferguson construes Fanny as part of the slavery discourse but argues that she "can ... always exercise choice" (1993, 72) and she "willingly cooperat[es] in her own assimilation" (73). It is in these moments of so-called "acquiescence," however, that we can witness Fanny's internalization of her oppression. Other critics make light of Fanny's situation, allying themselves with the parental figures who humiliate Fanny "for her own good."[9] Jane Nardin

---

9 This brings to mind Alice Miller's statement about responses to Kafka in *Thou Shalt Not Be Aware: Society's Betrayal of the Child* (1984): "When we hear that a writer had an unhappy childhood, we frequently attribute his or her artistic achievement to early traumatization. This view seems particularly applicable to Kafka, in whose works an exploitative society takes over the role of the parents, with the philosophy common to both being summed up in the words: 'The beating was good for you (us)'" (242). In a similar way, interpretations of Fanny's suffering as "character-building" reproduce the exploitation she experiences in the novel.

asserts that Fanny's "timidity and self-doubt ... which are a response to continual censure, seem a reasonable price to pay for the strong conscience that even the unfair discipline she received has nurtured in her" (1983, 83). While Paula Cohen admits that Fanny initially experiences "neglect and abuse at the hands of family members" (1993, 69), the novel has "a utopic ending" (60). Austen's "interest ... is an ideal of family that does not accommodate the self": Fanny Price's "selfhood ... is ultimately merged with the (male) other – with Edmund, with Sir Thomas – and they, by the end, have merged with her: all pain is transformed into pleasure, all difference into resemblance" (83). In short, all is forgiven.

Joan Klingel Ray provides a notable exception in her examination of Fanny as an "insightful study of 'the battered-child syndrome'" (1991, 16). While Ray's perceptive article discusses the emotional and physical abuse of Fanny, it does not include the issue of sexual abuse, nor does it recognize that the abuse of Fanny is integral to the value structure of Mansfield Park, that it cannot be isolated and contained in the hands of "the selfish Mrs Norris" (20). Ray scapegoats Mrs Norris and absolves the rest of the household, which is "ill-structured with the wrong person, the highly authoritative Mrs Norris, largely 'in charge.'" Ray argues that Sir Thomas and Lady Bertram, like Fanny's parents, are "well-meaning" and "basically unintentional, passive abusers" (18).

The colonization of Fanny's mind and body comes to a crisis in Henry Crawford's courtship of her. Sir Thomas is unable to comprehend her refusal and disobedience: it "requires explanation" (Austen 1988, 3:316). Indeed, given Fanny's schooling at Mansfield Park, her resistance is miraculous. The coercion to participate in the play *Lovers' Vows* was in a sense a rehearsal for the real challenge, Henry's proposal. Faced with a disobedient subject, Sir Thomas tries the usual means of persuasion. Echoing Mrs Norris's refrain of "considering who and what she is" (147), Sir Thomas manipulates Fanny's sense of obligation. After all, Henry Crawford "has been doing *that* for your brother, which I should suppose would have been almost sufficient recommendation to you, had there been no other" (316). He accuses Fanny of being "wilful and perverse" and charges that "the advantage or disadvantage of your family – of your parents – your brothers and sisters – never seems to have had a moment's share in your thoughts on this occasion. How *they* might be benefited, how *they* must rejoice in such an establishment for you – is nothing to *you*. You think only of yourself" (318). He asks Fanny if her "heart can acquit ... [her] of *ingratitude*," even though she does not "owe" him "the duty of a child" (319). Poor Fanny "did feel almost ashamed of herself, after such a picture as her uncle had drawn, for not liking Mr Crawford" (316).

Much to Fanny's dismay, Edmund is "entirely on his father's side of the question" (335): he "recommended there being nothing more said to her" and that "every thing should be left to Crawford's assiduities, and the natural workings of her own mind" (356). Sir Thomas's decision to send her to Portsmouth – the "medicinal project upon his niece's understanding" (369) – clearly demonstrates that Fanny is not "left to ... the natural workings of her own mind"; as John Wiltshire points out, the "medical metaphors suggest how coercion disguises itself in the mask of kindness" (1992, 101). Sir Thomas hopes "that a little abstinence from the elegancies and luxuries of Mansfield Park, would bring her mind into a sober state, and incline her to a juster estimate of the value of that home of greater permanence, and equal comfort, of which she had the offer" (Austen 1988, 3:369). The exile to Portsmouth is a repressive act of expulsion presented as a favour to Fanny, who indeed "was delighted" (369).

Unlike the other central heroines, Fanny has grown up away from her natural home. It is true that Austen heroines go away for a certain short time and this is often when crucial education takes place (Elizabeth Bennet's travels to Derbyshire and Pemberley; the Dashwoods' London stay; and Anne Elliot's visit to Uppercross, Lyme, and Bath), but these journeys are only temporary. Even in *Northanger Abbey*, though the majority of the action takes place away from the heroine's home, the home is still a fixed presence and one that welcomes Catherine's return once General Tilney rudely dismisses her from the abbey. Emma Woodhouse, the most socially and economically secure of all the heroines, never seems to go

anywhere: a day-trip to Box Hill is the extent of her travels. Fanny
Price, on the other hand, is permanently uprooted. Fanny is a heroine of displacement and orphanlike dependence and insecurity.
She leaves her natural home for a new one; when she later returns
to Portsmouth, she goes with all the sentiments of "going home"
but is sadly disappointed.

Fanny hopes that "to be at home again, would heal every pain
that had since grown out of the separation" (370), but her return
to Portsmouth reveals that "home" as just another site of neglect.
Portsmouth is "the very reverse of what she could have wished"
(388). Moira Ferguson interprets Fanny's disenchantment with
Portsmouth as her assimilation into Mansfield; she "rather coldly
rejects her origins" (1993, 83); she has "come to resemble the Eu-
rocentrically conceived 'grateful Negro' in pre-abolition tales who
collaborated with kind owners and discouraged disobedience
among rebel slaves" (74). Ferguson's reading overlooks the neglect
suffered by Fanny in the parental home. Nowhere else in Austen's
mature novels does a heroine think of her parents in such harsh
terms; even the foolish and heartless Sir Walter Elliot is protected
by daughterly loyalty. The Portsmouth home is reminiscent of the
outrageous family portraits we find in Austen's juvenilia; for example in "Jack and Alice," Alice's "whole Family are indeed a sad
drunken set" (Austen 1988, 6:23).

Fanny considers that Mr Price is "negligent of his family ... he
swore and he drank, he was dirty and gross" (3:389). Like Sir
Thomas, he objectifies and humiliates Fanny's body: "With an ac-
knowledgment that he had quite forgot her, Mr Price now received
his daughter; and, having given her a cordial hug, and observed
that she was grown into a woman, and he supposed would be wanting a husband soon, seemed very much inclined to forget her
again. Fanny shrunk back to her seat, with feelings sadly pained by
his language and his smell of spirits" (380). After that, Mr Price
"scarcely ever noticed her, but to make her the object of a coarse
joke" (389). Her mother fares little better: Fanny "might scruple to
make use of the words, but she must and did feel that her mother
was a partial, ill-judging parent, a dawdle, a slattern" (390). Indeed,

Sir Thomas's experiment works very well: "though her motives had been often misunderstood, her feelings disregarded, and her comprehension under-valued; though she had known the pains of tyranny, of ridicule, and neglect" (152), Fanny thinks back with fond nostalgia to Mansfield days. Going home also brings back her early childhood days of neglect: "She had never been able to recal anything approaching to tenderness in ... [her father's] former treatment of herself" (389).

Fanny's fantasy, "to be ... loved by so many, and more loved by all than she had ever been before, to feel affection without fear or restraint" (370), remains unfulfilled. Characteristically, Fanny blames herself: "She was at home. But alas! it was not such a home, she had not such a welcome, as – she checked herself; she was unreasonable. What right had she to be of importance to her family? She could have none, so long lost sight of! William's concerns must be dearest – they always had been – and he had every right ... *She* was only to blame" (382). As at Mansfield Park, Fanny feels unloved and insignificant, and due to the "privations ... she endured in her father's house" (413), "she had lost ground as to health since her being in Portsmouth" (409). John Wiltshire accurately describes Fanny's time in Portsmouth as "neglect and emotional isolation" (1992, 102). Sir Thomas, "had he known all, might have thought his niece in the most promising way of being starved, both mind and body, into a much juster value for Mr Crawford's good company and good fortune," but "he would probably have feared to push his experiment farther, lest she might die under the cure" (Austen 1988, 3:413).[10]

Fanny's exile is comparable to Marianne Dashwood's violent illness, a punitive and corrective period. Fanny "soon learnt to think with respect of her own little attic at Mansfield Park, in *that* house reckoned too small for anybody's comfort" (387). During her

10 See Douglas Murray's interesting article for an opposite view. He constructs Portsmouth as a positive place where Fanny takes on an active role and "for the first time ... participates without pain, without self-consciousness, in the system of public gazes that characterizes the Enlightenment" (1997, 21).

exile, Fanny learns to appreciate and to exercise class power. For the first time, she experiences the power and pleasure of giving, rather than the powerlessness and gratitude of receiving a gift. "So wholly unused to confer favours" (396), Fanny has the money to buy a second silver knife in order to settle an ongoing squabble between her sisters. The gift produces the same feelings in Susan that Mansfield "favours" had produced in Fanny: Susan "feared that her sister's judgment had been against her, and that a reproof was designed her for having so struggled as to make the purchase necessary for the tranquillity of the house," and she "blamed herself for having contended so warmly" (397). Fanny becomes a mentor to Susan. The new disseminator of knowledge, Fanny "became a subscriber ... in *propria persona*" (398) to the library, and prescribes a course of reading for Susan. Fanny indoctrinates her sister, preparing her as new material for consumption by Mansfield; indeed, Susan is later called to Mansfield to take Fanny's place.

Fanny is called back to Mansfield Park, once "this household of collapsed hopes" (Auerbach 1985, 31) is at the point of disintegration: Tom Bertram is very ill, Maria has left her husband, and Julia has run off with Mr Yates. When Mansfield Park is about to break down, ideological "house-cleaning" takes place. This involves the scapegoating and purging of the Crawfords, Maria, and Mrs Norris, whose "removal" was particularly of "great ... comfort" (Austen 1988, 3:465) to Sir Thomas: "He had felt her as an hourly evil ... she seemed a part of himself, that must be borne with for ever. To be relieved from her, therefore, was so great a felicity" (465–6). It is at this point that Sir Thomas thinks of retrieving Fanny: he is "not overpowered" and is "still able to think and act" (442). Rather than an "instance of his kindness" (443), his invitation to Fanny can be seen as an act of maintenance; for, after all, it is Fanny who continues the tradition of Mansfield Park. She "was indeed the daughter that he wanted": Sir Thomas's "charitable kindness had been rearing a prime comfort for himself. His liberality had a rich repayment" (472).

Once Fanny returns to Mansfield, the "least likely" and "morally impossible" (6) does happen: she marries Edmund. While it is true, as many are eager to point out, that marriage between first cousins was not considered incestuous in Austen's day, the relationship between Fanny and Edmund is constructed as fraternal: they have been "brought up ... always together like brothers and sisters" (6), and indeed, when Edmund turns to Fanny near the end of the novel, he calls her "my Fanny – my only sister – my only comfort now" (444).

The troublingly incestuous quality of the Edmund-Fanny marriage begs comment. Yet critics tend to explain it away, firmly dissociating it from the sexual. Nina Auerbach sees Fanny as "a literary monster ... a creature without kin who longs for a mate of her own kind" (1985, 34); her marriage to Edmund is Fanny's "cannibalistic invasion of the lighted, spacious estate of Mansfield" and "predatory victory" (28). Margaret Kirkham sees Fanny and Edmund's sibling relationship as ideal and Austen's way of criticizing the institution of marriage: Austen "shows that ... an ideal [equality] is more readily to be found, in contemporary society, between brothers and sisters than husbands and wives, though she seeks a transference to the marriage relationship of the ideal" (1987, 129). For Johanna Smith, "Their marriage is emblematic of this paralyzed retreat within the family, and proleptic of the nineteenth-century inescapable family." But she, too, evades the question of sexuality:

To define the incestuous overtones of [Fanny] and Edmund's relationship, we must move beyond a strictly sexual concept of incest to consider it first as an emotional relationship. Considered in this way, incest as I define it is "domestic" and "exclusive": domestic, because even in the absence of a literal sister-brother kinship (as in [Fanny] and Edmund's case), the relationship is *conceived* as fraternal; exclusive, because the intensity of such an affection tends to preclude romantic attachments outside the family. (1987, 2)

Similarly, Glenda Hudson, in *Sibling Love and Incest in Jane Austen's Fiction* (1992), defines incest as "a tightening of familial ties in an attempt to maintain traditional values in a rapidly changing *fin de siècle* world." Hudson is quick to point out that "the seeming fantasies of incestuous love and marriage are intended to provoke moral awareness rather than elicit immoral daydreams" (8), but she contradicts her argument that the unions are not sexual by stating that Austen "shows ... a potent and sympathetic love, a commingling of fraternal and erotic feelings, which, although the emphasis is very much on the former, we must recognize as a kind of incestuous love" (12).

Although Hudson may be alone in calling Fanny and Edmund "the blissful pair" (50), Auerbach, Kirkham, Cohen, and Smith all redefine the novel's incestuous marriage in non-sexual terms and thus elide the uncomfortable material that the text raises throughout. If Edmund and Fanny's incestuous union is not disturbing but, as Hudson reassures us, "positive and therapeutic" (9), then Sir Thomas's surveillance of Fanny's body also becomes harmless; the fact that it makes Fanny feel "quite oppressed" (Austen 1988, 3:178) is due to her natural timidity and we can agree with Edward that "it is but an uncle. If you cannot bear an uncle's admiration what is to become of you?" (198). These readings erase the history of violence; after all, it works out in the end and Fanny gets to marry Edmund.

Given Fanny's history of neglect and abuse at the great house, her inheritance of it is hardly a triumph, nor is it, as is so often argued, the climax of Austen's conservatism. Fanny and, by extension, *Mansfield Park* have often been seen as the embodiment of conservative values. Lionel Trilling states that the novel's "praise is not for social freedom but for social stasis. It takes full notice of spiritedness, vivacity, celerity, and lightness, but only to reject them" (1955, 211). Tony Tanner, calling *Mansfield Park* "The Quiet Thing" (1986, 142), describes it as "a stoic book" that "speaks for stillness rather than movement, firmness rather than fluidity, arrest rather than change, endurance rather than adventure" (173). For Edward Said, "Fanny Price (and Austen herself) finally subscribes" (1993, 62) to Sir Thomas's values. John Wiltshire argues that Fanny's "subjectivity ... replicates the structure of the social hierarchy which she inhabits": it is "as if the conservative social ideal of the eighteenth century moralists has met its perfect inhabitant" (1992, 94).

The marriage at the end of *Mansfield Park* is the closing example of Fanny's oppression. Fanny's love for Edmund is the result of her abuse. She reproduces the pattern of incest. She maintains the code of secrecy; for almost the entire novel, Fanny guards and hides a love that cannot be talked about. And she withdraws from the outside world, which she characterizes as hostile and unworthy. It is true that Fanny perpetuates the very ideology that has oppressed her, but her stillness is not one of reactionary conservatism: it is the stillness of somebody who is literally afraid to move.

That Austen turns this plot into a conventional marriage ending makes this her darkest novel; for it shows the violence underneath the surface of the institutions of family and marriage. On the surface, the novel indeed comes to a conservative resolution, but it simultaneously undermines that resolution by making us aware of the price that the aptly named Fanny Price has paid. In Claudia Johnson's words, the novel "never permits paternalistic discourse completely to conceal or to mystify ugly facts about power" (1988, 102). Mansfield Park's survival is dependent not only on the slave plantations, as recent criticism has shown, but also on the oppression of Fanny. Readers sometimes point out that life at Mansfield Park is surely preferable to life at Portsmouth, but such dubious logic comes dangerously close to Mrs Norris's.

Ironically, *Mansfield Park*'s ending has been interpreted as the overflowing of Austen's own family sentiments. Paula Cohen claims that "the ideal type of family experience … is a wish-fulfilment on the part of its author" (1993, 83): it is "the expression of a wish to remain anchored to the family of origin, to annex all needs to this nuclear family and close off all access and egress" (81). This supposedly "ideal … experience" (83) is a reflection of Austen's own life:

For Jane Austen, this is hardly a surprising wish. Living at home in a family that social conditioning had taught her to love above all else, having lost all hope of – or more correctly, having come to terms with a lack of desire for – marriage (we know that she received proposals and rejected them), Austen was also a member of a society that gave status only to married women. The logical solution to this double bind would be to marry inside the family, a wish approximately realized in her life through the role she acquired upon the death of her brother's wife a few years before she began writing*Mansfield Park*. At the same time, the structure and closure afforded by fiction provided her with a space in which this wish could be imaginatively depicted in the form of a perfectly closed nuclear family, uncontaminated by outside influences. (81)

   This quotation is a clear example of the circular logic that is employed in the effort to elide the uncomfortable material that *Mansfield Park* raises. The Fanny-Edmund marriage is a retreat from the corrupt world into the ideal family; within the "bosom of her own family" Jane Austen lived and wrote happily, "shrink[ing]" from the public world (Henry Austen 1988, 7). These two statements then become mutually reinforcing. Ultimately we know very little about her life. As Mary Poovey points out, Austen's letters are incomplete and "misleading" because of the "calculated editing Cassandra Austen performed on her sister's personal papers" (1984, xviii).[11] She argues that "hindsight" has been further "blurred" and "complicated ... by the officious concern of her relatives ... to beatify 'Aunt Jane'"(173), and ultimately to construe themselves in a flattering light. Poovey, however, draws on this "blurred ... hindsight" herself: "Jane Austen's experience of a close and supportive family ... provided [a] model ... for the way an individual's desires could be accommodated by social institutions"(203). David Nokes vividly demonstrates that the biographical facts can add up to a life of "family secrets" (1997, 9) and tensions far removed from the idealized Austen family portraits we find in earlier biographies. To explain away the incestuous ending of *Mansfield Park* by harking back to Austen's allegedly idyllic family life is a critical fallacy.
   Austen's novels are filled with absent or painfully inadequate parents – think of the intimidating General Tilney, the cruel Sir Walter

---

11 Deidre LeFaye claims that "close consideration shows that the destruction was probably because Jane had either described physical symptoms rather too fully ... or else because she had made some comment about other members of the family which Cassandra did not wish posterity to read" (1995, xv-xvi).

Elliot, the passive-aggressive Mr Woodhouse, even the delightfully sarcastic Mr Bennet. In *Persuasion*, Mrs Smith hesitates before revealing the "real character" (Austen 1988, 5:199) of Mr Elliot to Anne Elliot: "Even the smooth surface of the family-union seems worth perserving, though there may be nothing durable beneath" (198). Perhaps we as readers have been like Mrs Smith, attempting to preserve a "smooth surface" that will not hold. There has been a tendency to downplay the shortcomings depicted in the family portraits, but if we use *Mansfield Park* to counter-read the rest of Austen, we will begin to see the family album in a different light.

CHAPTER TEN

"*Unnatural and overdrawn*":
"*Alarming violence*" *in* Northanger Abbey

~

In *The Madwoman in the Attic*, Sandra Gilbert and Susan Gubar point out that "it was the harsh portrayal of the patriarch that most disturbed reviewers" about *Northanger Abbey*. They hint that it is due to the novel's depiction of domestic tyranny that Austen "could not find a publisher who would print it during her lifetime" (1979, 128); this view is echoed by Jacqueline Howard who writes that the novel "was suppressed by its first publisher" (1994, 181). The "Biographical Notice" attached to the posthumous publication of *Northanger Abbey* and *Persuasion* written by Austen's nephew Henry is, therefore, particularly interesting. An example of "the efforts ... to beatify 'Aunt Jane' for Victorian readers" (Poovey 1984, 173), the "Biographical Notice" stresses Jane Austen's family values, and it reveals the anxiety surrounding *Northanger Abbey*. Usually celebrated for its lighthearted parody, the novel explores domestic violence. My reading listens to Catherine and her suspicion that the general imprisoned and murdered his wife, thereby examining the representation of domestic violence in *Northanger Abbey* and in criticism of the novel.

Northanger Abbey contains Austen's famous vindication of the novel: "I will not adopt that ungenerous and impolitic custom so common with novel writers, of degrading by their contemptuous censure the very performances, to the number of which they are themselves adding" (Austen 1988, 5:37). The passage is indeed striking in its confidence; as Claudia Johnson remarks, "With very little ado, Austen proclaims the dignity of her genre as well as the authority of her own command over it – both at a time when such gestures were rare" (1988, 28). In the defence passage, Austen parodies readers who dismiss novels: "'I am no novel reader –

I seldom look into novels – Do not imagine that *I* often read novels – It is really very well for a novel.' – Such is the common cant. – 'And what are you reading, Miss –?' 'Oh! it is only a novel!' replies the young lady; while she lays down her book with affected indifference, or momentary shame" (Austen 1988, 5:37–8).[1] John Thorpe's disdain for novels is similar to that of the equally foolish Mr Collins in *Pride and Prejudice*, who "protested that he never read novels" (2:68). The defence passage in *Northanger Abbey* functions as a contract between Austen and the discriminating reader to take Catherine and the novel seriously, rather than dismiss them in the manner of the parodied reader.[2] In fact, Austen directs the very charges against novels, "effusions of fancy" (5:37), to ostensibly serious prose:

1 Showalter (1977) argues that "eighteenth-century women novelists exploited a stereotype of helpless femininity to win chivalrous protection from male reviewers and to minimize their unwomanly self-assertion" (17) and that "almost no sense of communality and self-awareness is apparent among women writers before the 1840s" (18). Austen's defence of women writers and novels in *Northanger Abbey* forms an important exception not noted by Showalter. We see this confidence already in Austen's juvenilia. Her dedication of "Catherine, or the Bower" is an interesting parody of the diffidence associated with the woman writer:

> Encouraged by your warm patronage of The beautiful Cassandra, and The History of England, which through your generous support, have obtained a place in every library in the Kingdom, and run through threescore Editions, I take the liberty of begging the same Exertions in favour of the following Novel, which I humbly flatter myself, possesses Merit beyond any already published, or any that will ever in future appear, except such as may proceed from the pen of Your Most Grateful Humble Servt The Author. (Austen 1988, 6:192)

As the note by Margaret Anne Doody and Douglas Murray points out, "only devotional works like *The Whole Duty of Man* went into so many editions in the eighteenth century ... No work of fiction could hope for such success" (Doody and Murray 1993, 346).

2 As Jacqueline Howard points out, "Austen's lengthy narratorial address has often been remarked, but seldom considered as contract with the reader and cue for interpreting other passages in the novel" (1994, 161). For Howard, the contract is about the novel's dialogic interaction with other discourses; it shows that, for example, Catherine's dislike of history should not be taken as her "untutored imagination" (174), for it is rather in accord with Austen's "reply to the mode of deprecatory critical discourse" in the defence passage (173). The idea of "contract with the reader" is a very valid one and in my reading, the defence passage functions as a contract stipulating that the reader take Catherine seriously.

Had the same young lady been engaged with a volume of the Spectator ... how proudly would she have produced the book, and told its name; though the chances must be against her being occupied by any part of that voluminous publication, of which either the matter or manner would not disgust a young person of taste: the substance of its papers so often consisting in the *statement of improbable circumstances, unnatural characters, and topics of conversation, which no longer concern any one living.* (38; emphasis added)

Austen sets up her novel in opposition to "improbable circumstances" and "unnatural characters" and announces it to be among those in which "the greatest powers of the mind are displayed, in which *the most thorough knowledge of human nature*, the happiest delineation of its varieties, the liveliest effusions of wit and humour are conveyed to the world in the best chosen language" (ibid.; emphasis added). By depreciating Catherine's suspicion about the general as "improbable," many readings of *Northanger Abbey* reproduce the very reader response that the defence passage attacks.

Catherine Morland has been seen as the quixotic heroine, who stumbles onto many a parodic disappointment. The young woman who reads too many novels for her own good is a common figure in eighteenth-century discourse, notably Arabella in Charlotte Lennox's *The Female Quixote* (1752). As Robert Uphaus succinctly describes this view, "Women are imitative readers who, evidently, tend to repeat in life what they read in fiction" (1987, 336). *Northanger Abbey* has been seen as part of this tradition. Obsessed with Gothic novels, Catherine expects life to be Radcliffian, and much of the novel's comedy occurs in the deflating of Catherine's expectations. For example, rather than the kind of incriminating death-bed note that Adeline discovers in Radcliffe's *The Romance of the Forest* (1791), disappointed Catherine finds only a laundry bill.[3] Similarly, the abbey is not what her imagination had painted: "the dif-

---

3 Gilbert and Gubar's point about the laundry bill is an interesting one: "Austen's heroine ... blunders on more significant, if less melodramatic, truths, as potentially destructive as any in Mrs Radcliffe's fiction ... Could Austen be pointing at the real threat to women's happiness when she describes her heroine finding *a laundry list?*" (1979, 135).

ference was very distressing" (Austen 1988, 5:162). The "dismal old weather-beaten" Lesley Castle in the fragment of the same name would have suited Catherine much better: "You can form no idea sufficiently hideous, of its dungeon-like form. It is actually perched upon a Rock to appearance so totally inaccessible, that I expected to have been pulled up by a rope" (Austen 1988, 6:123). Catherine's imaginings centre on General Tilney as the Gothic villain and culminate in the conjecture that he murdered his wife.

Some critics see Catherine's speculations about the general as the "most serious" (Devlin 1975, 44) of "her naive mistakes" (Litz 1965, 67). John Hardy describes Catherine's suspicions as her "house of Gothic cards," which inevitably "collapses" (1984, 14). During the course of the novel, Catherine learns to leave behind her literary exuberance and is chastened by the more reasonable hero.[4] D.D. Devlin argues that Catherine "is notoriously led astray by addiction to fiction" and "becomes temporarily blind to the real world of fact"; with the help of Henry Tilney, however, "she sheds her romantic blinkers and comes to see things as they are" (1975, 43). Critics such as Marilyn Butler, Litz, and Devlin interpret the novel as the disciplining of imagination: "The sympathetic imagination must be regulated; this is the sum of Catherine's education" (Litz 1965, 67).

Other scholars question this kind of reading. Lionel Trilling, in *The Opposing Self*, states that we are "quick, too quick" to see *Northanger Abbey* as "a snug conspiracy to disabuse the little heroine of errors of her corrupted fancy": Catherine "believes that life is violent and unpredictable. And that is exactly what life is shown to be by the events of the story: it is we who must be disabused of our belief that life is sane and orderly" (1955, 207). As critics like Trilling, Sandra Gilbert and Susan Gubar, Tony Tanner, and Claudia Johnson have pointed out, Catherine is right to distrust General

4 This critical account is similar to that found in many critiques of *Emma*, whose heroine is also scolded out of her quixotic tendencies by her lover-mentor. Susan Morgan's chapter "Guessing for Ourselves in *Northanger Abbey*" (1980) establishes a detailed connection between the two novels.

Tilney, and they examine the General's oppressive presence at home.[5] *Northanger Abbey* is not just a burlesque of Gothic fiction, at which we find Austen excels in the juvenilia: for example, "Henry and Eliza" compresses the cycle of pursuit, confinement, and escape characteristic of Radcliffe's novels into two pages of sheer burlesque (Austen 1988, 6:36–7). Austen "domesticates the gothic," Johnson argues, "and brings its apparent excesses into the drawing rooms of 'the midland countries [sic] of England'" (1988, 47). Johnson adds that while Henry Tilney, with "his conservative tendency to be pollyannaish about the *status quo*" (39), "dismiss[es] gothic novels as a 'good read'" (34), Jane Austen does not: "Austen may dismiss 'alarms' concerning stock gothic *machinery* – storms, cabinets, curtains, manuscripts – with blithe amusement, but alarms concerning the central gothic *figure*, the tyrannical father, she concludes, are commensurate to the threat they actually pose" (35). Jacqueline Howard argues that *Northanger Abbey* is "a self-reflexive unsettling of fixed notions of the real and the romantic" (1994, 169); its irony is directed not only at Catherine but also at Henry's "blinkered avowals of an ordered society and security from threat" (167). Although these critics give Catherine some credit, they simultaneously assert that she goes too far.

Some critics dismiss Catherine's imaginings about the general's capacity for violence altogether while others argue that her imaginations are "not that wide of the mark" (Johnson 1988, 40). Both camps agree, however, that Catherine's suspicions go too far. Yet there is a third way of reading *Northanger Abbey*. Domestic tyranny can extend to murder; while critics of *Northanger Abbey* compla-

---

5 Robert Hopkins's analysis firmly contextualizes *Northanger Abbey*, "perhaps the most political of Jane Austen's novels" (1978, 214), in specific "Affairs of State" (213). For example, the general's activities at night ("I have many pamphlets to finish … before I can close my eyes; and perhaps may be poring over the affairs of the nation for hours"; Austen 1988, 5:187) are seen as his "duties … as an inquisitor surveying possibly seditious pamphlets either for the Association for the Preservation of Liberty and Property or, after 1793, for the Home Office" (Hopkins 1978, 220). Also see Shinobu Minma's "General Tilney and Tyranny" (1996), according to which "Jane Austen believed that fundamentally the same mechanism was at work in the political world of both France and England in the 1790s" (510).

cently rule this out, the novel does not. Between the Gothic extreme (General Tilney as "Montoni"; Austen 1988, 5:187), which is parodied, and the domesticated gothic (General Tilney as "not perfectly amiable," 200) is a troubling possibility that the novel neither explicitly asserts nor explicitly denies: the euphemistic "crime of passion" of domestic violence.

Northanger Abbey does not give us any conclusive answers about Catherine's suspicion. The only "proof" of the general's innocence is delivered by Henry, who should not be confused with Austen, as he, like Mr Knightley, frequently is.[6] It is Catherine's word against Henry's. His famous speech is often considered the turning point in Catherine's process of education:

What have you been judging from? Remember the country and the age in which we live. Remember that we are English, that we are Christians. Consult your own understanding, your own sense of the probable, your own observation of what is passing around you – Does our education prepare us for such atrocities? Do our laws connive at them? Could they be perpetrated without being known, in a country like this, where social and literary intercourse is on such a footing; where every man is surrounded by a neighbourhood of voluntary spies, and where roads and newspapers lay every thing open? Dearest Miss Morland, what ideas have you been admitting? (197–8)

Henry's lecture produces the desired effect; Catherine feels "humbled": her "causeless terror ... had been all a voluntary, self-created delusion" (199). To see this passage as marking the movement from "fantasy to knowledge" (Devlin 1975, 28), however, is to assume General Tilney's innocence.

---

6 For example, Litz finds Austen's famous vindication of the novel "jarring" for "we have come to accept Henry Tilney as her spokesman": Henry's views "merge with those of his creator on so many occasions that we are disturbed when she speaks to us directly, or when Henry is suddenly subjected to her irony ... Jane Austen was experimenting in *Northanger Abbey* with several narrative methods she had not fully mastered, and the result is a lack of consistency in viewpoint" (1965, 69). This identification of Austen with the male hero is characteristic of criticism that looks at the heroine's flaw in the process of being corrected by the lover-mentor.

Henry's speech is a series of unanswered questions, and it does not settle anything. Henry is not the reliable witness he has been made out to be. First of all, he is hardly going to admit that his father murdered his wife, not just because of some sense of dysfunctional familial loyalty but, more important, because he shares some of his sister's fear of the general. When Catherine for the first time observes Henry in his father's presence, she is "puzzled": "instead of seeing Henry Tilney to greater advantage than ever, in the ease of a family party, he had never said so little, nor been so little agreeable" (Austen 1988, 5:129). Second, Austen shows Henry Tilney as an unreliable arbiter of Catherine's imagination because he encourages it in the first place. On the way to Northanger, Henry constructs a narrative of what Catherine might expect at the abbey. Catherine then proceeds to imagine precisely such adventures, and the comedy of the scene lies in the deflating of her expectations. Yet, as Catherine rightly points out, "it was in a great measure ... [Henry's] own doing, for had not the cabinet appeared so exactly to agree with his description of her adventures, she should never have felt the smallest curiosity about it"(173). At a later point, however, when Catherine's imagination takes off on its own rather than following Henry's Gothic formula, he tells her the exact opposite. Since he both incites gothic speculation and quenches it, his voice is highly suspect.

Further complicating any discussion of violence in the novel is the continual shifting of evaluative standards. The domestic tyranny that Austen does show is minimized by critics, who put it in the context of some larger, inadmissible act of violence. The general may silence Eleanor's speech and violate rules of gentility, but such acts pale in comparison to murdering or locking up a wife, which leaves the General merely a "petty tyrant" (Johnson 1988, 46). John Hardy argues, for example, that "the General's behaviour towards ... [Catherine] effectively gives the lie to Henry's remarks about the sane and even tenor of English life," at the same time stressing that "the enormity of what happens to Catherine should not be exaggerated" (1984, 16). Nowhere else in Austen's fiction do we see such a rude dismissal, except in the juvenilia. In

"Love and Freindship," MacDonald asks Laura and Sophia to "leave this House in less than half an hour," but they are guilty of theft and encouraging his daughter's elopement with an "unprincipled Fortune-hunter" (Austen 1988, 6:97). In "Evelyn," Mr Gower's response to the extraordinary generosity of the Webb family, who have given him their own land and home, is "You are welcome to stay this half hour if you like it" (183); here the rudeness serves to satirize the doctrine of sensibility. General Tilney violates rules of conduct and, forcing Catherine to travel alone, puts her in an unsafe situation. The seriousness of this violation is revealed by the response of Austen's contemporary, Maria Edgeworth: "The behaviour of the General ... packing off the young lady without a servant or the common civilities which any bear of a man, not to say gentleman, would have shown, is quite outrageously out of drawing and out of nature" (in Southam 1968, 17).

Critics tend to separate wife murder and "patriarchal tyranny," as if the two were unrelated. For example, Jacqueline Howard states that, contrary to Henry's opinion, "it is not the case that a concealed murder is unthinkable in Christian England, or that women are always safe," yet she simultaneously insists that "it is evident that Catherine's particular imaginings are wide of the mark" (1994, 167) and "bizarre." Howard goes on to say, however, that "after the misapprehensions have been cleared, Catherine has still had something real to fear and combat – patriarchal tyranny" (166). Again and again in the criticism of *Northanger Abbey*, the possibility that the general did kill his wife is represented as impossible. Yet there is overwhelming evidence in the text of the general's capacity for violence; hence we need to entertain the possibility of Catherine's being right.

Like that of Sir Thomas in *Mansfield Park*, General Tilney's presence is oppressive. Sir Thomas's return from Antigua puts an end to his children's carnival; the announcement "My father is come! He is in the hall at this moment," delivered by Julia with "a face all aghast" (Austen 1988, 3:172), dramatically concludes the second volume of *Mansfield Park*. General Tilney's presence has a similar effect, which initially "puzzled" Catherine: "It could not be General

Tilney's fault ... *He* could not be accountable for his children's
want of spirits, or for her want of enjoyment in his company"
(5:129). But soon Catherine's observations tell her that "*He*" is in
fact "accountable":

His departure gave Catherine the first experimental conviction that a loss
may be sometimes a gain. The happiness with which their time now passed,
every employment voluntary, every laugh indulged, every meal a scene of
ease and good-humour, walking where they liked and when they liked, their
hours, pleasures and fatigues at their own command, made her thoroughly
sensible of the restraint which the General's presence had imposed, and
most thankfully feel their present release from it. (220)

Frederick Tilney obviously is not fond of the family circle; having
been "lecture[d]" for "laziness" and "tardiness" (155, 154), he
"whisper[s]" to Eleanor, "How glad I shall be when you are all off"
(155). Catherine does not seem to blame him: "She was quite
pained by the severity of his father's reproof, which seemed disproportionate to the offence" (154–5). Henry's duties at Woodston
make Northanger "not more than half my home," and to Catherine's polite "How sorry you must be for that!" he pointedly replies,
"I am always sorry to leave Eleanor" (157).
   Eleanor does not have the avenues of escape that her brothers
luckily have. Aware of her situation, Henry is "sorry to leave" her at
the abbey with her father, but he does nothing to ease his sister's
situation. There is an overwhelming sense that Eleanor is aban-
doned or "solitary" (180) at the abbey. She admits, rather wistfully,
that "a mother would have been always present. A mother would
have been a constant friend; her influence would have been beyond all other" (180). Eleanor appears to be completely isolated,
and her "solitary" status implies vulnerability. We see glimpses of
the lack of freedom she experiences. General Tilney silences her
speech, monitors her company (he denies Catherine entrance to
the Bath residence and later throws her out of the abbey), and even
tries to regulate her movement ("Why do you chuse that cold,
damp path ... Our best way is across the park"; 179). General

Tilney's control over his daughter is firmly established; a "rather angrily" spoken word is enough to make her "dr[aw] back directly" (185) from showing Catherine her mother's apartment.

That Eleanor lives in fear is evident in her nervousness. For example, upon her arrival at the abbey, "Catherine found herself hurried away by Miss Tilney in such a manner as convinced her that the strictest punctuality to the family hours would be expected at Northanger" (162). Eleanor's "fear" and "alarm" are shown to be "not wholly unfounded, for General Tilney was pacing the drawing-room, his watch in his hand, and having, on the very instant of their entering, pulled the bell with violence, ordered 'Dinner to be on table *directly*!'" (165). Indeed, the word "violence" abounds in the novel; in chapter 6 of the second volume – significantly, the first chapter of Catherine's stay at the abbey – the word "violence" occurs seven times. The narrator dryly describes Eleanor's life at Northanger as "habitual suffering" (251).

Perhaps the focus of Catherine's concern should be the fate of Eleanor, rather than of Mrs Tilney. The connection between the two fates is evident in Eleanor's imitative worship of her mother: liking the walk she likes ("This is so favourite a walk of mine ... It was my mother's favourite walk"; 179), having her mother's portrait in her room, and visiting her mother's room. Of course, the already dead Mrs Tilney is a much safer avenue for speculation about General Tilney's capacity for violence, since, already dead and buried, she is distanced from the present and turned into a Gothic episode.[7]

With the exception of three chapters, the novel's action takes place away from the heroine's home at Fullerton. Catherine's consequent vulnerability, clearly evident in her expulsion from the abbey, is reminiscent of that of Fanny Price. Fanny may not have

7 Gilbert and Gubar offer a different interpretation: "Aspiring to become the next Mrs Tilney, Catherine is understandably obsessed with the figure of the last Mrs Tilney, and if we take her fantasy seriously, in spite of the heavy parodic tone here, we can see why, for Mrs Tilney is an image of herself. Feeling confined and constrained in the General's house, but not understanding why, Catherine projects her own feelings of victimization into her imaginings of the General's wife" (1979, 141).

shared Catherine's passion for "rolling down the green slope at the back of the house" (14), but she does share Catherine's mobility under pressure. Like Fanny, Catherine finds herself coerced by the very people she should be able to trust; as Claudia Johnson puts it, "bullying ... is rampant" (1988, 36) in *Northanger Abbey*. First, she is "whisked" away by John Thorpe against her wishes: "Catherine, angry and vexed as she was, having no power of getting away, was obliged to give up ... and submit" (87). Like Fanny, Catherine finds herself asked to submit to a "sacrifice [which] is not much" (99) by her brother: "I did not think you had been so obstinate, Catherine ... you were not used to be so hard to persuade; you once were the kindest, best-tempered of my sisters" (99–100). The coercion escalates to physical restraint; she is "caught hold of" (100), but finally she is able to "br[eak] away" (101). Her "resistance" is reminiscent of Fanny's refusal to take part in the play; both are motivated by a "conviction of being right" (101) and both are coerced by the very people they trust.

After Henry Tilney humiliates Catherine into seeing the error of her ways, she never again dares to contemplate the possibility of the general's having murdered his wife. Catherine's thoughts no longer are her own – she too has become a prisoner of Northanger Abbey. As Paul Morrison argues, Catherine is "enclosed in openness" by the end: "the principle of her claustration" is "not in an economy of gothic secrecy, but in a domestic sphere, at once social and psychological, in which there are no secret spaces, in which there is no escape from an openess that encloses" (1991, 12). But the fact that Catherine's question stays unanswered is significant, revealing *Northanger Abbey*'s ambiguous representation of domestic violence. That the novel raises uncomfortable suggestions is evident in the critical energy spent on wholly or partly discrediting Catherine. *Northanger Abbey*, if read monologically from the perspective of the "reasonable" Henry Tilney, certainly allows one to do so, but as this reading has shown, the text in its entirety is not limited to Henry's perspective. *Northanger Abbey* leaves it to the reader to determine the extent of the general's violence.

CHAPTER ELEVEN

"This ill-used girl, this heroine of distress": The "Diabolical scheme" in Lady Susan

~

In her foreword to *Jane Austen's Beginnings: The Juvenilia and* Lady Susan, Margaret Drabble writes, "These sketches provide an excellent antidote to the conventional view of Jane Austen as a calm, well-mannered novelist, confined to a narrow social world of subtle nuance and at times crippling decorum." Often, however, this "antidote" is not administered. While celebrating the daring quality of *Lady Susan,* Drabble herself insists that it "remains an isolated, an alarming creation, from another fictional universe" (1989, xiv). Indeed, *Lady Susan* has often been considered as an extraterrestrial visitation on the Austen landscape. As Hugh McKellar puts it, "For the peace of mind of all concerned, Lady Susan had to be declared a cuckoo in the Austen nest, with her existence explicable only on the assumption that her creator had not yet put away childish things" (1989, 206). The anomalous nature of *Lady Susan,* however, has been overstated.

When Frederica arrives at Churchill, Mrs Vernon "never saw any creature look so frightened in my life" (Austen 1988, 6:269). Mrs Vernon believes that Lady Susan "has no real Love for her daughter & has never done her justice, or treated her affectionately": "She [Lady Susan] hardly spoke to her, & on Frederica's bursting into tears as soon [as] we were seated, took her out of the room & did not return for some time; when she did, her eyes looked very red, & she was as much agitated as before. We saw no more of her daughter" (270). "Perfectly timid, dejected & penitent" (270), Frederica is isolated from the rest of the family under the pretence of her playing the pianoforte for the "great part of the day" in Lady Susan's dressing-room: "*practising* it is called, but I seldom hear any noise when I pass that way. What she does with herself there I do not know" (271). When the unwanted suitor, Sir James Martin, arrives, Frederica is "as pale as ashes" and "terrified" (275). Frederica's beleaguered state is similar to that of Fanny Price, as is her determined resistance in the face of coercion: "I would rather work for my bread than marry him" (279).

Margaret Drabble points out that Lady Susan "has now, predictably, been adopted by some feminist critics as an example of a 'free woman,' unhindered by the usual concepts of female and more particularly maternal duty" (1989, xiv). Lady Susan, however, imprisons Frederica, and she is not different from the oppressive patriarchal power of Sir Thomas in *Mansfield Park*. When Sir Thomas is faced with Fanny's opposition, he sends her back to Portsmouth: "a little abstinence from the elegancies and luxuries of Mansfield Park, would bring her mind into a sober state" (Austen 1988, 3:369). Similarly, Lady Susan refrains from "so harsh a measure" as "forc[ing] Frederica into a marriage from which her heart revolted" (Austen 1988, 6:253) but decides to make the marriage Frederica's "own choice by rendering her life thoroughly uncomfortable till she does accept him" (253–4). To this effect, Lady Susan sends Frederica away to school and discourages Mrs Johnson's offer to visit her there: "I hope to see her the wife of Sir James within a twelvemonth. You know on what I ground my hope, & it is certainly a good foundation, for School must be very humiliating to a girl of Frederica's age; and by the bye, you had better not invite her any more on that account, as I wish her to find her situation as unpleasant as possible" (253). Sir Thomas and Lady Susan have the same aim: to manipulate their dependent into a marriage that will suit their own needs. This selfish motivation is illustrated very clearly when Lady Susan ends up marrying Sir James herself.

Mrs Vernon describes Lady Susan as having "a happy command of Language, which is too often used I believe to make Black appear White" (251). As Barbara Horwitz points out, Lady Susan employs conduct-book discourse to "justify her behaviour": she "is quite conscious of her ability to appropriate the language of those whose ideas she has no notion of accepting" (1989, 183). The epistolary form illuminates the discrepancy between Lady Susan's avowed parental concern and her real desire to control her daughter. For example, when Frederica runs away, Lady Susan admits to Mrs Johnson that her "horrid" daughter "*shall* be punished, she *shall* have him" (268), but she acts the conscientious parent to Mrs Vernon: "It will be absolutely necessary … as you my dear Sister must be sensible, to treat my daughter with some severity while she is here; – a most painful necessity, but I will endeavour to submit to it. I am afraid I have been too often indulgent, but my poor Frederica's temper could never bear opposition well. You must support & encourage me. – You must urge the necessity of reproof, if you see me too lenient" (267).

Sir Thomas Bertram also disguises his agenda in the language of familial affection, much as Lady Susan does. To send Fanny on a visit to Portsmouth "had occurred to Sir Thomas, in one of his dignified musings, as a right and desirable measure." He discusses it with Edmund who "considered it every way, and saw nothing but what was right" (Austen 1988, 3:368), but Sir Thomas has "views of good over and above what he had communicated to his son." His "prime motive" (369) is not, of course, "dignified." Although Lady Susan's and Sir Thomas's forms of behaviour are very similar, their kinship has not been acknowledged. Lady Susan is seen as the "Wicked Mother" (Horwitz 1989, 181), the aberrant character in Austen, while Sir Thomas is misguided, but "well-meaning" (Ray 1991, 18): he is "(up to a point) just, benevolent and responsible" (Tanner 1986, 151).

When Lady Susan is almost found out by Mrs Vernon, she tries to vindicate herself by asking with incredulity:

Good God! … what an opinion must you have of me! Can you possibly suppose that I was aware of her unhappiness? that it was my object to make my child miserable, & that I had forbidden her speaking to you on the subject, from a fear of your interrupting the Diabolical scheme? Do you think me destitute of every honest, every natural feeling? Am I capable of consigning *her* to everlasting Misery, whose welfare it is my first Earthly Duty to promote? (Austen 1988, 6:289)

The response to this is clearly affirmative. But while Mrs Vernon tells Frederica that her mother "has no right to make you unhappy" (287), she and Reginald's parents are equally embroiled in the "Diabolical scheme." The characterization of Lady Susan as evil is necessary for the legitimization of De Courcy's authority. The text does not limit its questioning of parental figures to Lady Susan. A dark portrayal of authority and manipulation, *Lady Susan* shows Frederica and Reginald finally to be just pawns in the war between Lady Susan and the De Courcy family.

When Sir Reginald De Courcy is alarmed at the possibility of his son's marriage to Lady Susan, his response is presented in the language of familial affection and obligation: "Everything [is] at stake; your own happiness, that of your Parents, and the credit of your name … I do not wish to work on your Fears, but on your Sense & Affection" (260–1). Finally, however, he is no less harsh than Lady Susan. Admitting that "it is out of my power to prevent your inheriting the family Estate" and claiming that "my ability of distressing you during my Life, would be a species of revenge to which I should hardly stoop under any circumstances," Sir Reginald outlines precisely such a course of conduct: "It would destroy every comfort of my Life, to know that you were married to Lady Susan Vernon. It would be the death of that honest Pride with which I have hitherto considered my son, I should blush to see him, to hear of him, to think of him" (261).

Sir Reginald's wrath does not need to be executed; the family crisis is averted, as events conspire to expose Lady Susan. Reginald is saved from Lady Susan's machinations, however, only to fall prey to his sister's and mother's schemes: "Frederica runs much in my thoughts, & when Reginald has recovered his usual good spirits (as I trust he soon will), we will try to rob him of his heart once more, & I am full of hopes of seeing their hands joined at no great distance" (309). The piece closes when Reginald De Courcy finally "could be talked, flattered & finessed into an affection for" Frederica, "which, allowing leisure for the conquest of his attachment to her mother, for his abjuring all future attachments & detesting the Sex, might be reasonably looked for in the course of a Twelvemonth" (313).

Northanger Abbey "leave[s] it to be settled by whomsoever it may concern, whether the tendency of this work be altogether to recommend parental tyranny, or reward filial disobedience" (Austen 1988, 5:252). *Lady Susan* does not give the reader such a choice; it clearly states that Lady Susan "has no right to make" Frederica "unhappy" (Austen 1988, 6:287). It is a dark family portrait, relentlessly exposing the family as a site of power and coercion. This is a topic common to all of the novels, and *Lady Susan* deserves its rightful place in Austen's *oeuvre*.

What, or who, is Jane Austen?

~

In "What Is an Author," Michel Foucault argues that Saint Jerome's "four principles of authenticity" for establishing the biblical canon "define the critical modalities now used to display the function of the author" (1986, 144):

The texts that must be eliminated from the list of works attributed to a single author are those inferior to the others (thus, the author is defined as a standard level of quality); those whose ideas conflict with the doctrine expressed in the others (here the author is defined as a certain field of conceptual or theoretical coherence); those written in a different style and containing words and phrases not ordinarily found in the other works (the author is seen as a stylistic uniformity); and those referring to events or historical figures subsequent to the death of the author (the author is thus a definite historical figure in which a series of events converge). (Ibid.)

We see these principles at work in the constructions of Jane Austen. One striking feature of Austen criticism is the frequent insistence that a particular novel is the most didactic, or the weakest, or the most different from the others. Each novel, in turn, has been seen as the exception. Congruous with the fixing of a particular novel as "exceptional" is the notion of the "flawed" novel that deviates from the standard of the perfect Austen novel. Yet, as with the case of the "exception," almost every novel has been considered "flawed" to some degree.

Northanger Abbey is an immature work that suffers from internal inconsistencies and is separated from the rest of the novels because it is mainly a burlesque: "From any approach, *Northanger Abbey* remains the least satisfying of Austen's novels, and the slightest in emotional and moral content" (Fergus 1983, 14). *Sense and Sensibility* is deeply flawed by the heavy-handed contrast between the two sisters; it "is the most obviously tendentious of Jane Austen's novels, and the least attractive" (Marilyn Butler 1987, 195), and "most readers would agree that ... [it] is the least interesting of Jane Austen's works" (Litz 1965, 72). *Mansfield Park* is problematic because of its unlikeable heroine: "Nobody, I believe, has ever found it possible to like the heroine of *Mansfield Park*" (Trilling 1955, 212), Thomas Edwards's "Difficult Beauty of *Mansfield Park*" (1987, 7). *Persuasion* is radically different from the other novels in its Romantic consciousness and disillusionment with the social order: in "none" of the other novels "does Jane Austen have to deal with the painful realisation that the social order which it has been the business of her literary career to explore and vindicate is finally falling apart" (Monaghan 1980, 162); the novel presents a "Brave New World" (Auerbach 1985, 39). *Pride and Prejudice* is exceptional; for "in no other novel, not even in *Emma*, would Austen allow us to believe that structures of authority could be assailed without irreparably tarnishing their luster" (Johnson 1988, 93). That leaves us with *Emma*. If all the novels are exceptions, then what is the normative novel? In other words, what is the consistency that constitutes an *oeuvre*? This leads to the Foucauldian question "What, or who, is the author Jane Austen?" The anxiety surrounding this question is revealed by the insistent attempt to define her.

I have avoided a chronological examination of the novels in order to undermine the narrative of "progress" from the "early" to the "mature" novels that Austen criticism often imposes. Duckworth, for example, argues that "to turn from *Mansfield Park* to a consideration of *Northanger Abbey* and *Sense and Sensibility* is to move back in terms of chronology of composition and *down in terms of literary quality*" (1994, 82; emphasis added). I have discussed the novels in conjunction with each other and with the juvenilia, to point out similarities; *Lady Susan*, with which I conclude, offers a particularly vivid illustration of constructions of the author. *Lady Susan* does not seem to "fit" because its "evil" main character is not in accord with Jane, who never experienced "even for a moment, an abatement of good-will from any who knew her" (Henry Austen 1988, 5:3), and who in her writing "always sought, in the faults of others, something to excuse, to forgive or forget. Where extenuation was impossible, she had a sure refuge in silence" (6). The definition of *Lady Susan* as aberrant has been further legitimized in terms of its form. None of the mature works are written as epistolary fiction; *Sense and Sensibility* and *Pride and Prejudice* started as series of letters but were rewritten. Parts of the juvenilia, notably "Love and Freindship" and "Lesley Castle," are composed in epistolary form; hence *Lady Susan*'s convenient exile into this marginalized category of *Minor Works*. Hugh McKellar insists with exasperation that we need to "grapple with the possibility that the little story [*Lady Susan*] is not trying to be *Emma* and failing, but trying to be something quite different – and succeeding" (1989, 206). In my reading, *Lady Susan* shares common territory with *Mansfield Park* and *Northanger Abbey*; it is not *Lady Susan* who is different, but Jane Austen.

David Musselwhite argues that readings of Emily Brontë's *Wuthering Heights* are often limited because they wilfully ignore what he calls the "unacceptable text" of *Wuthering Heights*. "What is daunting," he claims, "... is the sheer weight of the established tradition and the strategies with which it perpetuates itself" (1977, 154). Austen scholarship is also shaped by the "sheer weight of the established tradition." Roger Sales offers an assessment, at times scathing, of the reproductions of Jane Austen and the Regency in contemporary British culture and the conservative purpose these reproductions serve:[1] a "fantasy of total perfection is projected

---

1 Sales cites the British Jane Austen Society as a particular example but states that the "bracketing together" of the British and North American Jane Austen Societies "does a disservice" to the latter: "Its journal, *Persuasions*, shows a healthy interplay between the pleasures of the fan club and a concern to promote historically informed critical readings. The English one, by contrast, has always been deeply suspicious of most forms of literary and historical criticism" (1994, 15).

back onto the Regency period so that it becomes a safe haven that is completely uncontaminated by what are taken to be the vulgarities of the modern world" (1994, 20).

North American examples of this construction can be seen in *Victoria* magazine, which frequently alludes to eighteenth- and nineteenth-century literature. The magazine used *Mansfield Park* to advertise bedding: "Like the private chambers of Fanny, the heroine in Jane Austen's 'Mansfield Park,'" the bedroom above – outfitted with sheets, comforter, and dust ruffle from Ralph Lauren's Spectator Collection – is a warm "nest of comforts" ("The Romantic English woman," 22). Unheated, Fanny's room (and, by extension, her life) is hardly the warm nest of comforts that *Victoria* has construed it to be. It ignores the fact that Fanny's room signals her marginal status within the Mansfield family and that it actually betrays her economic and social deprivation. Formerly inhabited by the governess, it is a room that "nobody else wanted": "what had been originally plain, had suffered all the ill-usage of children – and its greatest elegancies and ornaments were a faded footstool of Julia's work, too ill done for the drawing-room" and "a collection of family profiles thought unworthy of being anywhere else" (Austen 1988, 3:151, 152). Much criticism of *Mansfield Park* parallels this erasure of the material reality, although using different strategies. The cover-up is easily identifiable in *Victoria* magazine, as is its agenda, but should not be taken lightly. As Sales warns us, "It would be very arrogant indeed to assume that all those who teach or study Austen are necessarily exempt from, rather than implicated in, th[e] cultural process" (1994, 26).

In Musselwhite's reading of *Wuthering Heights*, "there is evidence that that unread and outcast text has remained to haunt and trouble the cosiness of conventional readings, tapping, like the waif Catherine, on a shuttered consciousness" (1977, 155). The "cosiness" of the readings of Austen is similarly threatened by elements of the novels – what I have called the "other" heroine, the "narrative cameo," and "investigating crimes" – that the critical tradition has defensively labelled as "flaws." All three paradigms have explored violence, becoming more and more explicit, as we move along the continuum from the silencing of voice to sexual abuse and, finally, murder. Harriet Smith's exile in Brunswick Square on account of a "tooth" being "amiss" (Austen 1988, 4:451) represents an act of coercion necessary to the main narrative in the same manner that Fanny's oppression is integral to the value system of Mansfield Park. These are some of Austen's "unacceptable texts."

I have tried to expand the space that Jane Austen inhabits in traditional criticism by presenting readings that fully acknowledge the dialogism of Austen's texts and its implications. Foucault states that the author's "function ... is to characterize the existence, circulation, and operation of certain discourses within a society" (1986, 142). I have used Bakhtin's theories of dialogism to challenge the received author-function of Jane Austen, and to release some of her texts' "unresolvable dialogues" (Bakhtin 1981, 291).

"Another world must be unfurled"
Austen Country

~

In measured verse I'll now rehearse
  The charms of lovely Anna:
And, first, her mind is unconfined
  Like any vast savannah.

Ontario's lake may fitly speak
  Her fancy's ample bound:
Its circuit may, on strict survey
  Five hundred miles be found.

Her wit descends on foes and friends
  Like famed Niagara's Fall;
And travellers gaze in wild amaze,
  And listen, one and all.

Her judgment sound, thick, black, profound,
  Like transatlantic groves,
Dispenses aid, and friendly shade
  To all that in it roves.

If thus her mind to be defined
  America exhausts,
And all that's grand in that great land
  In similes it costs –

Oh how can I her person try
   To image and portray?
How paint the face, the form how trace
   In which those virtues lay?

Another world must be unfurled,
   Another language known,
Ere tongue or sound can publish round
   Her charms of flesh and bone.

"In measured verse I'll now rehearse" was written by Jane Austen
for her niece, Anna Lefroy. In *A Memoir of Jane Austen* (1886),
J.E. Austen-Leigh introduces the poem in a rather dismissive manner: "Once, too, she took it into her head to write the following
mock panegyric on a young friend" (89). His commentary continues in a pejorative manner, denying any serious artistic intention
on Austen's part: "I believe that all this nonsense was nearly extem-
pore, and that the fancy of drawing the images from America arose
at the moment from the obvious rhyme which presented itself in
the first stanza" (90). Chapman, who included the poem in his edition of the *Minor Works*, titles the poem with J.E. Austen-Leigh's description of it as a "Mock Panegyric on a Young Friend" (Austen
1988, 6:442). Margaret Anne Doody and Douglas Murray (1993),
however, respect Jane Austen's own words ("In measured verse I'll
now rehearse"), rather than her nephew's.

I choose to read the poem not as a "mock panegyric" but as a joyful celebration of the female "mind," "fancy," "wit," and "judgment
sound." The poem is a suitable conclusion to this journey through
Austen's work. The journey began with Adrienne Rich's poem,
"Aunt Jennifer's Tiger," in which the "proud and unafraid" tigers
"pranc[e]" in a vastness of space sharply in contrast with Aunt Jennifer's "ringed" existence. The vastness that forms the subtext to
Aunt Jennifer's needlework comes to the foreground in "In measured verse I'll now rehearse." The poem is startlingly different
from the alleged narrowness of Austen's art, her "little bit (two
Inches wide) of Ivory" (Austen 1995, 323). Here, Austen's look

encompasses the "vast savannah," "Ontario's lake" with a "circuit" of "Five hundred miles," "Niagara's fall" and "transatlantic groves." But even the new world is not enough for this yearning spirit: "her mind to be defined / America exhausts." The poem gestures towards an unchartered language:

> Another world must be unfurled,
>   Another language known,
> Ere tongue or sound can publish round
>   Her charms of flesh and bone.

This is the Austen I have tried to produce.

Bibliography

Adams, Hazard, and Leroy Searle. *Critical Theory Since 1965*. Tallahassee,
  FL: Florida State University Press, 1986.
Althusser, Louis. *Lenin and Philosophy and Other Essays*. Translated by Ben
  Brewster. London: New Left Books, 1971.
Armstrong, Nancy. *Desire and Domestic Fiction: A Political History of the Novel*.
  New York: Oxford University Press, 1987.
Auerbach, Nina. *Romantic Imprisonment: Women and Other Glorified Outcasts*.
  New York: Columbia University Press, 1985.
Austen, Henry. "Biographical Notice of the Author." In Jane Austen.
  Northanger Abbey and Persuasion. Vol. 5 of *The Novels of Jane Austen*, edited
  by R.W. Chapman, 3–9. 6 vols. 3d ed. Oxford: Oxford University Press,
  1988.
Austen-Leigh, J.E. *A Memoir of Jane Austen*. 6th ed. London: Bentley, 1886.
Austen, Jane. *Catherine and Other Writings*. Edited by Margaret Anne Doody
  and Douglas Murray. Oxford: Oxford University Press, 1993a.
– *The History of England: From the Reign of Henry the 4th to the Death of Charles
  the 1st*. Chapel Hill: Algonquin, 1993b.
– *Jane Austen's Letters*. Edited by Deirdre Le Faye. 3d ed. Oxford: Oxford
  University Press, 1995.
– *The Novels of Jane Austen*. Edited by R.W. Chapman. 6 vols. 3d ed. Oxford:
  Oxford University Press, 1988.
Austen-Leigh, Joan. "The Juvenilia: A Family 'Veiw.'" In *Jane Austen's Begin-
  nings: The Juvenilia and Lady Susan*, edited by J. David Grey, 173–9. Ann
  Arbor: UMI Research Press, 1989.
Austen-Leigh, William, and Richard Arthur Austen-Leigh. *Jane Austen: A
  Family Record*. [1913] Edited by Deidre Le Faye. Rev. ed. London: British
  Library, 1989.

Backscheider, Paula R. Introduction. In Elizabeth Inchbald. *The Plays of Elizabeth Inchbald.* 2 vols. vol. 1, ix-xxxvii. New York: Garland, 1980.

Baer, Marc. *Theatre and Disorder in Late Georgian London.* Oxford: Clarendon, 1992.

Bakhtin, Mikhail. *The Dialogic Imagination.* Edited by Michael Holquist. Translated by Caryl Emerson and Michael Holquist. Austin: University of Texas Press, 1981.

– *Problems of Dostoevsky's Poetics.* Edited and translated by Caryl Emerson. Minneapolis: University of Minnesota Press, 1984.

Baldridge, Cates. *The Dialogics of Dissent in the English Novel.* Hanover: University Press of New England, 1994.

Barker, Francis, ed. *Literature, Society and the Sociology of Literature.* Essex: University of Essex Press, 1977.

Bauer, Dale M. *Feminist Dialogics: A Theory of Failed Community.* Albany: State University of New York Press, 1988.

Bauer, Dale M., and Susan Jaret McKinstry, eds. *Feminism, Bakhtin, and the Dialogic.* Albany: State University of New York Press, 1991.

Belsey, Catherine. *Critical Practice.* London: Routledge, 1980.

Bennett, Paula. "Family Plots: *Pride and Prejudice* as a Novel about Parenting." In *Approaches to Teaching Austen's* Pride and Prejudice, edited by Marcia McClintock Folsom, 134–9. New York: Modern Language Association, 1993.

Bilger, Audrey. *Laughing Feminism: Subversive Comedy in Frances Burney, Maria Edgeworth, and Jane Austen.* Detroit: Wayne State University Press, 1998.

Bloom, Harold, ed. *Jane Austen's* Mansfield Park. New York: Chelsea, 1987.

Booth, Wayne C. Introduction. In Mikhail Bakhtin. *Problems of Dostoevsky's Poetics.* Edited and translated by Caryl Emerson, xiii-xxvii. Minneapolis: University of Minnesota Press, 1984.

Brantlinger, Patrick. *The Rule of Darkness: British Literature and Imperialism, 1830–1914.* Ithaca: Cornell University Press, 1988.

Brown, Julia Prewitt. *Jane Austen's Novels: Social Change and Literary Form.* Cambridge: Harvard University Press, 1979.

Brownmiller, Susan. *Against Our Will: Men, Women and Rape.* New York: Simon and Schuster, 1975.

Butler, Marilyn. *Jane Austen and the War of Ideas.* 1975. Oxford: Clarendon, 1987.

Butler, Sandra. *Conspiracy of Silence: The Trauma of Incest.* 1978. San Francisco: Volcano, 1985.

Byatt, A.S. Introduction. In Jane Austen. *The History of England,* v-viii. Chapel Hill: Algonquin, 1993.

Castellanos, Gabriela M. *Laughter, War and Feminism: Elements of Carnival in Three of Jane Austen's Novels.* New York: Peter Lang, 1994.

Chandler, Alice. "'A Pair of Fine Eyes': Jane Austen's Treatment of Sex." *Studies in the Novel* 7 (1975): 88–103.

Chapman, R.W. Introduction. In Jane Austen. *Jane Austen's Letters to Her Sister Cassandra and Others.* 2d ed. London: Oxford University Press, 1964.

Churchill, Winston J. *Closing the Ring.* New York: Houghton Mifflin, 1951.

Clark, Anna. *Women's Silence, Men's Violence: Sexual Assault in England 1770–1845.* London: Pandora, 1987.

Cleland, John. *Memoirs of a Woman of Pleasure.* Edited by Peter Sabor. Oxford: Oxford University Press, 1985.

Cohen, Paula Marantz. *The Daughter's Dilemma: Family Process and the Nineteenth-Century Domestic Novel.* Ann Arbor: University of Michigan Press, 1993.

Devlin, D.D. *Jane Austen and Education.* London: Macmillan, 1975.

Doody, Margaret Anne. Introduction. In Jane Austen. *Sense and Sensibility.* Oxford: Oxford University Press, 1990.

Doody, Margaret Anne, and Douglas Murray. Notes. In Jane Austen. *Catherine and Other Writings.* Edited by Margaret Anne Doody and Douglas Murray. Oxford: Oxford University Press, 1993.

Drabble, Margaret. Foreword. In *Jane Austen's Beginnings: The Juvenilia and Lady Susan,* edited by J. David Grey, xiii-xiv. Ann Arbor: UMI Research Press, 1989.

Duckworth, Alistair M. *The Improvement of the Estate: A Study of Jane Austen's Novels.* 1971. Rev. ed. Baltimore: Johns Hopkins University Press, 1994.

Edwards, Thomas R. "The Difficult Beauty of *Mansfield Park.*" In *Jane Austen's* Mansfield Park, edited by Harold Bloom, 7–21. New York: Chelsea, 1987.

Evans, Mary. *Jane Austen and the State.* London: Tavistock, 1987.

Fergus, Jan. *Jane Austen and the Didactic Novel.* New York: Barnes and Noble, 1983.

Ferguson, Moira. *Colonialism and Gender Relations from Mary Wollstonecraft to Jamaica Kincaid: East Caribbean Connections.* New York: Columbia University Press, 1993.

Foucault, Michel. "What is an Author?" In *Critical Theory Since 1965,* edited by Hazard Adams and Leroy Searle, 138–48. Tallahassee, FL: Florida State University Press, 1986.

Fraiman, Susan. "The Humiliation of Elizabeth Bennet." In *Refiguring the Father: New Feminist Readings of Patriarchy,* edited by Patricia Yaeger and Beth Kowaleski-Wallace, 168–87. Carbondale: Southern Illinois University Press, 1989.

– "Peevish Accents in the Juvenilia: A Feminist Key to *Pride and Prejudice.*" In *Approaches to Teaching Austen's* Pride and Prejudice, edited by Marcia McClintock Folsom, 74–80. New York: Modern Language Association, 1993.

Gard, Roger. *Jane Austen's Novels: The Art of Clarity.* New Haven and London: Yale University Press, 1992.

Gibbon, Frank. "The Antiguan Connection." *Cambridge Quarterly* 11, 2 (1982): 298–305.

Gilbert, Susan M., and Susan Gubar. *The Madwoman in the Attic: The Woman Writer and the Nineteenth-Century Literary Imagination.* New Haven: Yale University Press, 1979.

Gilbert, Susan M., and Susan Gubar, eds. *The Norton Anthology of Literature by Women: The Tradition in English.* New York: Norton, 1985.

Goldsmith, Oliver. *The Vicar of Wakefield.* [1766] New York: Signet, 1982.

Greene, Donald. "The Myth of Limitation." In *Jane Austen Today,* edited by Joel Weinsheimer, 142–75. Athens, GA: University of Georgia Press, 1975.

Grey, David J., ed. *Jane Austen's Beginnings: The Juvenilia and* Lady Susan. Ann Arbor: UMI Research Press, 1989.

Gross, Sybil Gloria. "Flights into Illness: Some Characters in Jane Austen." In *Literature and Medicine during the Eighteenth Century,* edited by Marie Mulvey Roberts and Roy Porter, 188–99. London: Routledge, 1993.

Halperin, John. *The Life of Jane Austen.* Sussex: Harvester, 1984.

– "Unengaged Laughter: Jane Austen's Juvenilia." In *Jane Austen's Beginnings: The Juvenilia and* Lady Susan, edited by J. David Grey, 29–44. Ann Arbor: UMI Research Press, 1989.

Hardy, John. *Jane Austen's Heroines: Intimacy in Human Relationships.* London: Routledge and Kegan Paul, 1984.

Heilbrun, Carolyn G. *Writing a Woman's Life.* New York: Ballantine, 1988.

Hennessy, Rosemary. *Materialist Feminism and the Politics of Discourse.* New York: Routledge, 1993.

Herman, Edward, and Noam Chomsky. *Manufacturing Consent: The Political Economy of the Mass Media.* New York: Pantheon, 1988.

Herman, Judith Lewis. *Father-Daughter Incest.* Cambridge: Harvard University Press, 1981.

Hodge, Jane Aiken. *The Double Life of Jane Austen.* London: Hodder and Stoughton, 1972.

Hohne, Karen, and Helen Wussow, eds. *A Dialogue of Voices: Feminist Literary Theory and Bakhtin.* Minneapolis: University of Minnesota Press, 1994.

Holquist, Michael. *Dialogism: Bakhtin and His World.* London: Routledge, 1990.

Honan, Park. *Jane Austen: Her Life.* New York: St Martin's, 1987.

Hopkins, Robert. "General Tilney and Affairs of State: The Political Gothic of *Northanger Abbey.*" *Philological Quarterly* 57 (1978): 213–24.

Horwitz, Barbara. "Lady Susan: The Wicked Mother in Jane Austen's Work." In *Jane Austen's Beginnings: The Juvenilia and* Lady Susan, edited by J. David Grey, 181–91. Ann Arbor: UMI Research Press, 1989.

Howard, Jacqueline. *Reading Gothic Fiction: A Bakhtinian Approach.* Oxford: Clarendon, 1994.

Hudson, Glenda A. *Sibling Love and Incest in Jane Austen's Fiction.* New York: St Martin's, 1992.

Husbands, H. Winifred. "*Mansfield Park* and *Lovers' Vows*: A Reply." *Modern Language Review* 29 (1934): 176–79.

Hutcheon, Linda. *The Canadian Postmodern: A Study of Contemporary English-Canadian Fiction.* Toronto: Oxford University Press, 1988.

Inchbald, Elizabeth. *Lovers' Vows.* 1798. In Jane Austen. *The Novels of Jane Austen.* Edited by R.W. Chapman, vol. 3, 475–538. 3d ed. Oxford: Oxford University Press, 1988.

– *The Plays of Elizabeth Inchbald.* 2 vols. New York: Garland, 1980.

Jarrett-Kerr, Martin. "The Mission of Eng. Lit." Letter in the *Times Literary Supplement* (3 February 1984): iii.

Jenkins, Elizabeth. *Jane Austen: A Biography.* London: Gollancz, 1938.

Johnson, Claudia L. *Jane Austen: Women, Politics, and the Novel.* Chicago: University of Chicago Press, 1988.

– "'The Kingdom at Sixes and Sevens': Politics and the Juvenilia." In *Jane Austen's Beginnings: The Juvenilia and* Lady Susan, edited by J. David Grey, 45–58. Ann Arbor: UMI Research Press, 1989.

– "What Became of Jane Austen? *Mansfield Park.*" *Persuasions: Journal of the Jane Austen Society of North America* 17 (1995): 59–70.

Jordan, Elaine. "Pulpit, Stage, and Novel: *Mansfield Park* and Mrs. Inchbald's *Lovers' Vows.*" *Novel* 20 (1987): 138–48.

Kavanagh, James H. "Ideology." In *Critical Terms for Literary Study,* edited by Frank Lentricchia and Thomas McLaughlin, 306–20. Chicago: University of Chicago Press, 1990.

Kent, Christopher. "Learning History with, and from, Jane Austen." In *Jane Austen's Beginnings: The Juvenilia and* Lady Susan, edited by J. David Grey, 59–72. Ann Arbor: UMI Research Press, 1989.

Kirkham, Margaret. "Feminist Irony and the Priceless Heroine of *Mansfield Park.*" In *Jane Austen's* Mansfield Park, edited by Harold Bloom, 117–33. New York: Chelsea, 1987.

– *Jane Austen, Feminism and Fiction.* Sussex: Harvester, 1983.

Kronenberger, Louis. *The Polished Surface: Essays in the Literature of Worldliness.* New York: Knopf, 1969.

Lee, Ang, dir. *Sense and Sensibility.* Columbia Pictures, 1995.

Le Faye, Deidre. "A Note on the Text." In Jane Austen. *The History of England,* ix–xii. Chapel Hill: Algonquin, 1993.

– Preface to The Third Edition. In Jane Austen. *Jane Austen's Letters.* Edited by Deidre Le Faye. 3d. ed. Oxford: Oxford University Press, 1995.

Lennox, Charlotte. *The Female Quixote.* Edited by Margaret Dalziel. Oxford: Oxford University Press, 1989.

Lentricchia, Frank, and Thomas McLaughlin, eds. *Critical Terms for Literary Study.* Chicago: University of Chicago Press, 1990.

Lew, Joseph. "'That Abominable Traffic': *Mansfield Park* and the Dynamics of Slavery." In *History, Gender & Eighteenth-Century Literature,* edited by

Beth Fowkes Tobin, 271–300. Athens, GA: University of Georgia Press, 1994.

Litz, A. Walton. *Jane Austen: A Study of Her Artistic Development.* New York: Oxford University Press, 1965.

Lodge, David. *After Bakhtin: Essays on Fiction and Criticism.* London: Routledge, 1990.

MacDonagh, Oliver. *Jane Austen: Real and Imagined Worlds.* New Haven: Yale University Press, 1991.

MacKenzie, Henry. *The Man of Feeling.* London: Oxford University Press, 1967.

McKellar, Hugh. "*Lady Susan*: Sport or Cinderella." In *Jane Austen's Beginnings: The Juvenilia and* Lady Susan, edited by J. David Grey, 205–14. Ann Arbor: UMI Research Press, 1989.

McClintock, Marcia, ed. *Approaches to Teaching Austen's* Pride and Prejudice. New York: Modern Language Association, 1993.

McMaster, Juliet. "The Children in *Emma.*" *Persuasions: Journal of the Jane Austen Society of North America* 14 (1992): 62–7.

– *Jane Austen on Love.* Victoria: English Literary Studies, 1978.

– "The Talkers and Listeners of *Mansfield Park.*" *Persuasions: Journal of the Jane Austen Society of North America* 17 (1995): 77–89.

– "Teaching 'Love and Freindship.'" *Jane Austen's Beginnings: The Juvenilia and* Lady Susan, edited by J. David Grey, 135–51. Ann Arbor: UMI Research Press, 1989.

McMaster, Juliet, and Bruce Stovel, eds. *Jane Austen's Business: Her World and Her Profession.* London: Macmillan, 1996.

Mezei, Kathy, ed. *Ambiguous Discourse: Feminist Narratology and British Women Writers.* Chapel Hill: University of North Carolina Press, 1996.

Michell, Roger, dir. *Persuasion.* BBC Films, 1995.

Miller, Alice. *Thou Shalt Not Be Aware: Society's Betrayal of the Child.* Translated by Hildegarde and Hunter Hannum. 1984. New York: Meridian, 1990.

Miller, D.A. *Narrative and Its Discontents: Problems of Closure in the Traditional Novel.* Princeton: Princeton University Press, 1981.

Minma, Shinobu. "General Tilney and Tyranny: *Northanger Abbey.*" *Eighteenth-Century Fiction* 8 (1996): 503–18.

Moi, Toril. *Sexual/Textual Politics: Feminist Literary Theory.* London: Routledge, 1988.

Moler, Kenneth. *Jane Austen's Art of Allusion.* Lincoln: University of Nebraska Press, 1968.

Monaghan, David. *Jane Austen: Structure and Social Vision.* London: Macmillan, 1980.

Morgan, Susan. "Emma Woodhouse and the Charms of Imagination." *Studies in the Novel* 7 (1975): 33–48.

– *In the Meantime: Character and Perception in Jane Austen's Fiction.* Chicago: University of Chicago Press, 1980.

Morrison, Paul. "Enclosed in Openness: *Northanger Abbey* and the Domestic Carceral." *Texas Studies in Literature and Language* 33 (1991): 1–23.

Mudrick, Marvin. *Jane Austen: Irony as Defense and Discovery.* Princeton: Princeton University Press, 1952.

Mukherjee, Meenakshi. *Jane Austen.* London: Macmillan, 1991.

Murray, Douglas. "Spectatorship in *Mansfield Park*: Looking and Overlooking." *Nineteenth-Century Literature* 52 (1997): 1–26.

Musselwhite, David. "*Wuthering Heights*: The Unacceptable Text." In *Literature, Society and the Sociology of Literature*, edited by Francis Barker, 154–60. Essex: University of Essex Press, 1977.

Nardin, Jane. "Children and Their Families in Jane Austen's Novels." In *Jane Austen: New Perspectives*, edited by Janet Todd, 73–87. New York: Holmes and Meier, 1983.

Neill, Edward. "The Politics of 'Jane Austen.'" *English* 29 (1991): 205–13.

– *The Politics of Jane Austen.* Basingstoke: MacMillan, 1999.

Newton, Judith Lowder. *Women, Power and Subversion: Social Strategies in British Fiction, 1778–1860.* New York: Methuen, 1981.

Nokes, David. *Jane Austen: A Life.* Berkeley: University of California Press, 1997.

Perera, Suvendrini. *Reaches of Empire: The English Novel from Edgeworth to Dickens.* New York: Columbia University Press, 1991.

Perry, Ruth. "Austen and Empire: A Thinking Woman's Guide to British Imperialism." *Persuasions: Journal of the Jane Austen Society of North America* 16 (1994): 95–106.

Poovey, Mary. *The Proper Lady and the Woman Writer: Ideology as Style in the Works of Mary Wollstonecraft, Mary Shelley, and Jane Austen.* Chicago: University of Chicago Press, 1984.

Radcliffe, Ann. *The Romance of the Forest.* Oxford: Oxford University Press, 1986.

Radway, Janice A. *Reading the Romance: Women, Patriarchy, and Popular Literature*. Chapel Hill: University of North Carolina Press, 1984.

Ray, Joan Klingel. "Jane Austen's Case Study of Child Abuse: Fanny Price." *Persuasions: Journal of the Jane Austen Society of North America* 13 (1991): 16–26.

Reitzel, William. "*Mansfield Park* and *Lovers' Vows*." *Review of English Studies* 9 (1933): 451–6.

Rich, Adrienne. *The Fact of a Doorframe: Poems Selected and New, 1950–1984*. New York: Norton, 1984.

Roberts, Marie Mulvey, and Roy Porter, eds. *Literature and Medicine during the Eighteenth Century*. London: Routledge, 1993.

"The Romantic Englishwoman." *Victoria* 9, no. 3 (March 1995): 22.

Roulston, Christine. "Discourse, Gender, and Gossip: Some Reflections on Bakhtin and *Emma*." In *Ambiguous Discourse: Feminist Narratology and British Women Writers*, edited by Kathy Mezei, 40–65. Chapel Hill: University of North Carolina Press, 1996.

Sabor, Peter. "'Staring in Astonishment': Portraits and Prints in *Persuasion*." In *Jane Austen's Business: Her World and Her Profession*, edited by Juliet McMaster and Bruce Stovel, 17–29. London: Macmillan, 1996.

Said, Edward W. *Culture and Imperialism*. New York: Knopf, 1993.

Sales, Roger. *Jane Austen and Representations of Regency England*. London: Routledge, 1994.

Seeber, Barbara K. "'I See Every Thing As You Desire Me to Do': The Scolding and Schooling of Marianne Dashwood." *Eighteenth-Century Fiction* 11 (1999): 223–33.

Seeber, Barbara K., and Kathleen James-Cavan. "'Unvarying, warm admiration every where': The Truths about Wentworth." *Persuasions: Journal of the Jane Austen Society of North America* 16 (1994): 39–47.

Shaffer, Julie Andrea. "Confronting Conventions of the Marriage Plot: The Dialogic Discourse of Jane Austen's Novels." Doctoral dissertation, University of Washington, 1989. Ann Arbor: University Microfilms International, 1989. 9006995.

– "The Ideological Intervention of Ambiguities in the Marriage Plot: Who Fails Marianne in Austen's *Sense and Sensibility*?" In *A Dialogue of Voices: Feminist Literary Theory and Bakhtin*, edited by Karen Hohne and Helen Wussow, 128–51. Minneapolis: University of Minnesota Press, 1994.

Showalter, Elaine. *A Literature of Their Own: British Women Novelists from Brontë to Lessing.* Princeton: Princeton University Press, 1977.

Smith, Johanna M. "'My only sister now': Incest in *Mansfield Park.*" *Studies in the Novel* 19 (1987): 1–15.

Southam, B.C. *Jane Austen: The Critical Heritage.* London: Routledge and Kegan Paul, 1968.

– "The Silence of the Bertrams: Slavery and the Chronology of *Mansfield Park.*" *London Times Literary Supplement,* 17 February 1995, 13–14.

Spencer, Jane. *The Rise of the Woman Novelist: From Aphra Behn to Jane Austen.* Oxford: Basil Blackwell, 1986.

Tanner, Tony. *Jane Austen.* London: Macmillan, 1986.

Tave, Stuart M. *Some Words of Jane Austen.* Chicago: University of Chicago Press, 1973.

Thompson, Emma. *Sense and Sensibility: The Screenplay and Diaries.* London: Bloomsbury, 1995.

Tobin, Beth Fowkes, ed. *History, Gender and Eighteenth-Century Literature.* Athens, GA: University of Georgia Press, 1994.

Todd, Janet, ed. *Jane Austen: New Perspectives.* New York: Holmes and Meier, 1983.

Tomalin, Claire. *Jane Austen: A Life.* New York: Knopf, 1997. London: Penguin, 1998.

Trilling, Lionel. *The Opposing Self.* New York: Viking, 1955.

Troost, Linda, and Sayre Greenfield, eds. *Jane Austen in Hollywood.* Lexington: University of Kentucky Press, 1998.

Uphaus, Robert W. "Jane Austen and Female Reading." *Studies in the Novel* 19 (1987): 334–45.

Vendler, Helen. *The Odes of John Keats.* Cambridge: Harvard University Press, 1983.

Watt, Ian. Introduction. In *Jane Austen: A Collection of Critical Essays,* edited by Ian Watt, 1–14. Englewood Cliffs: Prentice-Hall, 1963.

Weinsheimer, Joel, ed. *Jane Austen Today.* Athens, GA: University of Georgia Press, 1975.

Wiltshire, John. *Jane Austen and the Body.* Cambridge: Cambridge University Press, 1992.

Wordsworth, William. *Selected Prose.* Harmondsworth: Penguin, 1988.

Yaeger, Patricia. *Honey-Mad Women: Emancipatory Strategies in Women's Writing.* New York: Columbia University Press, 1988.

Yaeger, Patricia, and Beth Kowaleski-Wallace. *Refiguring the Father: New Feminist Readings of Patriarchy.* Carbondale: Southern Illinois University Press, 1989.

Zietlow, Paul. "Luck and Fortuitous Circumstances in *Persuasion*: Two Interpretations." *English Literary History* 32 (1965): 179–95.

Index